MAGICAL MIDLIFE SHIFT

BARBARA'S SASSY MIDLIFE TALES

MILLY TAIDEN

Published By
Latin Goddess Press
Winter Springs, FL 32708
http://millytaiden.com
Magical Midlife Shift
Copyright © 2022 by Milly Taiden
Cover: Jacqueline Sweet

❀ Created with Vellum

Old dogs can definitely learn new tricks, and so can wise witches.

Sara Walters has spent her time teaching other witches about the magical ways, but now that she's fifty and it's time for her to retire, she's not sure what to do with herself. When she meets a sexy suitor her world is turned upside down. She's supposed to act like an adult, but that's a tall order when he makes her feel so young and carefree.

Rhett Armstrong had long ago decided he would be happy being a lifelong bachelor until one scenting ceremony brings him what he thought he'd never find: his fated mate. She's the picture of beauty, strength and sass. And he wouldn't have her any other way.

Though Sara thought she knew everything there was to know about herself, it turns out there are still secrets hidden within, and a certain wolf shifter is the key to them coming to the surface. But then he makes her question if they could really ever work. **Now, she's out of time and has to decide between listening to her heart or focusing on her fears.**

MAGICAL MIDLIFE SHIFT

BARBARA'S SASSY MIDLIFE TALES

NEW YORK TIMES and USA TODAY
BESTSELLING AUTHOR
MILLY TAIDEN

—For my readers who can relate to an older heroine and love reading their stories,

Enjoy this sweet and sexy midlife romance.

CHAPTER ONE

"Are you sure about this makeup?" Sara asked her new apprentice, Vera.

The young, twenty-something woman beamed at Sara in the mirror. "I'm absolutely sure. You look fabulous."

Sara couldn't argue. After her salon day, her grey-streaked, black hair looked brighter and bouncier, and now, after Vera's makeup job, Sara's face looked ten years younger.

For her part, Sara had never seen her eyes lined and her lashes thickened, and she'd *never* applied such a pink shade of lipstick.

But she was about to embark on a new chapter in her life, so she figured, why not allow her new apprentice to glam her up a bit?

"Alright, come on now. Your guests await!" Vera urged Sara toward the door.

Before stepping down the stairs, she took a deep breath. This was *her* party, and it was just as important as any graduation or sweet-sixteen.

This was the party being held in honor of her transition from a teacher at the witch academy to her new career running a witch Bed and Breakfast and being a local witch mentor.

It was the mid-life change for her kind.

She'd already moved into the huge Victorian home, which had been fully furnished and decorated by the mentor witches who'd occupied it before her. Vera Yang had greeted her, having already started her apprenticeship under the previous witch.

At least that was one thing Sara had. A friend and somewhat of a guide in Vera, though it was Sara who was supposed to be the mentor.

The partnership worked well. Sara would help Vera with her magic, and Vera would help Sara get used to living life outside the academy, which had been the only life Sara had known ever since she'd entered it as a student when she was still just a child.

The crowd of people cheered for Sara as she

stepped onto the main floor. Sara smiled and waved, seeing some faces she knew and many she didn't.

They were the paranormal leaders of nearby town groups, shifters, and other covens.

Audry Ewing, the current academy headmistress, was waiting for her. She waved Sara over. "Well, Sara, here we are! I never thought that we'd see this day when I met you all those years ago."

Sara hardly did either. She'd figured she would have stayed at the academy forever, moving from teacher to administration as she'd aged out.

But something had called her to take a chance on something different, and when the previous witch who'd lived here passed, Sara saw it as a sign. She needed to try something different.

Audry went on, telling the guests about Sara's achievements as she introduced her to the new community she'd serve. But Sara could hardly hear her. She was busy looking at all the people she was about to meet, feeling both nervous and excited.

No longer would she live at the academy and be on call twenty-four seven, but now, she would have her own home and be on her own for the first time since before she became a student and then a teacher.

After Audry finished her speech, Sara walked with Vera around the room, shaking hands with everyone.

"Sara, this is Barbara Wolfe," Vera said, guiding her over to a woman around Sara's age but with the kindest eyes Sara had ever seen.

She shook hands with Barbara. "I'm the matriarch of the Wolf pack in Blue Creek."

"Nice to meet you," Sara said, wishing she had more time to chat with the woman.

Much later in the evening, when she thought the last guest, and even Vera, had left, she spotted Barbara on the couch in the living room.

"You stayed!" Sara said.

"I wanted a chance to talk to you a bit more," Barbara revealed.

Honestly, Sara didn't mind because she could see wanting to get to know Barbara, too. Something inside Sara made her feel like she would be a great friend.

"This was a lovely party," Barbara said.

"Oh, well, I didn't have much to do with it," Sara said demurely. "Vera, Audry, and Monet put it all together. All I'd been doing was moving myself from the academy and getting used to my new surroundings."

Sara offered Barbara a refill on her glass of wine and topped off her own too. Then she sat down on the couch with the wolf shifter.

"I love this house," Sara sighed. The Victorian-style home came fully furnished, which was good since Sara had no furniture of her own, but she also looked forward to making the place feel more like *her.*

"It is very lovely. Large, too."

"That it is! I'm going to need a cat." Sara laughed. "It's far too quiet when everyone leaves."

"Soon enough, you'll have people coming in and out. I'm sure it won't be quiet for long."

Barbara was right. The four-bedroom home served as a Bed and Breakfast for traveling witches and sometimes a boarding home for witches who had yet to settle in their new permanent location.

Soon enough, Sara wouldn't be alone.

"I can't believe how much they cleaned up before they left," Sara mused aloud. "And here I thought I'd at least be able to do some of that. I don't know what I'm going to do to keep myself busy while I'm waiting for bookings."

"Surely you'll have many people stopping in to meet you," Barbara reasoned.

"Perhaps, but I think most of them were here

tonight," Sara said. "And I already met the local coven at my initiation ceremony."

Barbara smiled understandingly. "Well, if you'd like a chance to get to know some of the local shifters, we have a Scenting Ceremony coming up."

"What's that?" Sara asked.

"It is an annual tradition, a ceremony my husband Tristan and I host. The young wolves in our pack and other packs gather, hoping to find their fated mate."

"Ah!" Though I didn't have much experience with shifters, I did know about their fated mate sense. It was the magic they each had that activated when they met the one they were meant to spend their life with. "They wouldn't mind an outsider being present at such a sacred event?"

"Of course not," Barbara assured her. "Not when you're personally invited by me."

Sara's tablet notifications chirped, which she realized it may have been doing all night, but she hadn't heard it over the noise of the party-goers.

"Sorry," Sara said, quickly pulling the device out of the drawer in her coffee table. The home screen was filled with notifications for the dating sight she'd signed up for on a whim the night before. "Oh jeez, I forgot I'd even signed up for that last night."

Embarrassed, she tried to hide it from Barbara, but it was too late.

Barbara didn't judge her, though. "Dating now that you're out and free from the academy? Good for you!"

"I don't know. I thought maybe I should start putting myself out there some, you know? Not that we weren't allowed to date while working at the academy, but they don't allow married witches to teach, so I'd never involved myself in anything serious that could put me in a situation where I had to choose between a man and the job I loved."

"Is that part of why they force retirement at fifty?" Barbara asked. "To force you to get out there and live a little?"

"Maybe," Sara shrugged. "It has a lot to do with their insistence that rollover is good for the school, good for education and progress, but yeah. It's an early age for retirement, and I still have a lot of life to live."

"And love to give," Barbara added.

Sara nodded. "But I'm not sure I want to jump into a relationship or love or anything like that. I think I'm just looking for a night out here or there. Or maybe occasional companionship." Sara said.

"Occasional companionship? What exactly do you mean by that?" Barbara smiled conspiratorially with Sara, clearly understanding exactly what Sara meant.

"You know what I mean." Sara blushed.

Barbara nudged her. "You mean … sex? As in, you want to get laid?"

Sara giggled like a schoolgirl. "Yeah, yeah, that's what I meant."

Barbara laughed right along with her and then motioned toward the tablet. "I'm always curious what kind of guys are on the dating sites. Tristan and I have been together since before those things existed. Can I see?"

Sara handed over the tablet, her profile visible for Barbara to view.

"Your idea of a great date is dinner and a long walk on the beach." Barbara read. "You sure you want to say that when there aren't many beaches around here?"

"Hmmm," Sara took the device back, editing that answer. "How about dinner and a long walk through the park?" She adjusted her answer to suit the geographic area.

"And you left that one blank," Barbara said, pointing to 'What's the first thing you notice about a guy? His arms, his ass, his package?'

"I forgot to put anything there. I was just so shocked that there are women who actually check out a guy's … you know … right off the bat." Sara laughed, typing 'eyes' for her answer.

"Nice," Barbara replied. "It's not what I would pick, but eyes is a good answer."

"Does that mean you're a package lady then?"

"Arms." Barbara didn't even bother looking up from the device.

"Why arms?" Sara asked.

"Because big strong arms are great for holding you down and …"

They dissolved into giggles again.

"And what about shifters? Would you date a shifter?" Barbara asked.

"Would that even work?" Sara looked at Barbara inquisitively. "I mean … don't shifters only want to date other shifters?"

"Some, but not all. Particularly those at our age, who aren't thinking about the need to make shifter babies." Barbara said.

"Well, then yeah. I mean, I don't personally have an issue with a shifter. I just figured they wouldn't want to date a witch. Wait, is there a box for that question?"

"No. I was just curious to see what you would say." Barbara chuckled. "Now, about this photo. Is it your professional headshot?"

"Yeah, it is." Sara blushed. "I like it, but I guess it's a little formal for a dating site. I should probably take new photos."

"Let's do it!"

"What, now?"

Barbara nodded. "You look gorgeous right now, so why not?"

Sara considered. "My apprentice did glam me up tonight. It might be dumb to waste it. But I'm not good at …"

Barbara didn't give her a chance to finish. She took the tablet, put it in camera mode, and coached Sara through a photo session. After another glass of wine, they finally ended up in a profile pic they were both quite proud of.

"Send that to me," Barbara instructed. "I have many eligible people I know who I could show it to."

Sara hesitated.

Barbara tilted her head to the side. "What, you

don't trust me to show your pic to nice men I think might be a good match for you?"

"I just never had someone setting me up on dates before. I feel like I'm being a burden."

"Love is *never* a burden," Barbara emphasized. "Nothing makes me happier than helping two people find each other."

"Okay …" Sara hardly thought that was likely, but she took Barbara's phone number and texted the photo to her anyway.

As they were talking, another notification came in, chiming and then briefly showing a photo of the man who was interested in her profile.

"Oh, this one is kinda' cute."

That sparked Sara's interest. "Let me see."

Barbara tilted her tablet so Sara could see the image on the screen.

"No way! I might be a witch who enjoys the woods, but I don't think I want to be with a guy who looks like he lives there or might just be a sasquatch."

"Yeah, he does have that wild-man thing going on, doesn't he? Okay, fine. What about this one?" Barbara showed her another profile that had popped up.

"He's definitely hawwtt!" Sara suddenly felt the

need to fan herself. The man on the screen looked like he had just stepped off the pages of a Playgirl Magazine.

"He is definitely a silver fox if I ever saw one." Barbara did what Sara was thinking, fanned herself before clicking the heart next to his profile.

"What does adding that heart mean?" Sara asked.

"That you're interested," Barbara explained.

"Wait! I'm not sure if I'm interested. I said he was hot." Sara began to panic. "You really think someone as hot as him would be interested in someone like me? He looks all normal. I'm not normal. I'm a witch with hardly any experience in the real world, and I'm freaking out."

"Calm down. He may not even see the like."

Just as Barbara said that a little box popped up indicating the silver fox had sent a message.

Sara noted his name, Bryce, and then read his message:

Hi, beautiful.

"Okay … so maybe he did see it," Barbara said, handing Sara the tablet.

"What do I do?" she squeaked.

"Say hi back?"

Hi.

Sara wanted to unsend as soon as she sent the message.

"Well, I'm going to head out and let you talk to Mr. Silver Fox." Barbara stood and grabbed her purse.

"What! You can't leave me here to do this alone!" Sara shouted, jumping up off the couch.

"Sure, I can. You'll be fine. Just follow your gut and see where things go," Barbara said before giving Sara a hug.

"You got me into this, and now you're jumping ship! I can't believe this." Sara wasn't joking. She had no idea how to talk to guys. Well, not in a, *hey, I'm interested in you,* kind of way.

"You'll be fine. Just be yourself, and if Mr. Silver Fox isn't for you, move on to the next. Just remember that you don't owe these guys anything. Only talk to the ones you are comfortable with.

"Crap!" Rhett growled. He was running late for his lunch thanks to a client who had no understanding when it came to the law of physics and construction. Rhett couldn't install a giant soaker tub in a second-floor bathroom without first reinforcing the floor. What was so hard to understand about that, and why did the client think that arguing with him would change anything?

Now, thanks to said hardhead, Rhett had hardly any time to clean up before meeting Barbara and Tristan for lunch.

If there was one thing Rhett hated, it was being late.

The second he pulled into his driveway, he slammed his truck into park and hopped from the driver's seat. Rushing into the house, he peeled off his clothes as he sprinted for the bathroom. Turning the water to full blast, he hopped into the shower before the water even had a chance to warm up.

"Argh!" he shouted when the frigid water pelted his back. Goosebumps broke out over his skin. Determined to make it to dinner on time, Rhett didn't bother waiting for the water to warm up. Just as the water started to warm up, he finished with a shortened shower routine and jumped out.

Quickly toweling off, he ran a comb through his short hair and grabbed the first clean pair of jeans and t-shirt he could find. He found himself speeding out of his driveway toward the restaurant within five minutes. The directions they had given him were easy enough to follow, considering he was already familiar with the area.

Thank goodness, traffic was light, and he pulled up to the restaurant with five minutes to spare. Rhett flipped the visor down and popped open the mirror. Might as well try to tame a bit of his salt-and-pepper hair before he went in, now that he had a moment. He ran his finger through his hair, fixing a few strands that seemed to have minds of their own. Satisfied with the way he looked, he hopped from his truck.

Barbara and Tristan approached the restaurant door at the same time Rhett did. He greeted them, giving Tristan a handshake and Barbara a hug. It had been too long since he'd seen his former alpha and matriarch.

"How is life treating you out here?" Tristan asked once they were seated.

"Works good," Rhett replied. "But it's not till I see some old friendly faces that I realize how much I miss pack life."

"Watch who you're calling *old,*" Barbara admonished with a playful smile. "But you know you'd be welcome back any time you wanted to return."

Rhett shrugged. He'd been considering it far more than he was willing to admit. He'd focused so much of his young life on building his company that he never thought he'd be willing to just walk away from it someday.

"If you were thinking about semi-retirement, I know you'd be able to find some jobs to keep you busy if you brought your company to Blue Creek," Tristan said, almost reading his mind. "We have lots of people moving in all the time, and new builds are definitely in demand."

Rhett smiled, shaking his head. The Wolfes weren't subtle. It was clear they wanted him to move home. Was this why they invited him to lunch? To try to convince him to move home? "When you invited me to lunch, you didn't say why you were in town."

"We're just doing some tourism," Tristan said. At the same time, his wife said, "We're antiquing."

Right.

The waitress came by to take their orders. She was a pretty blond thing with a bouncy ponytail and soft makeup who started shamelessly flirting with Rhett, even giggling as she patted his arm before she took his menu from him.

As she walked away, Rhett shook his head, sighing regretfully. "They just keep getting younger and younger."

"Why, Rhett, you make it sound like you're finally sick of the bachelor's life," Barbara commented.

He shrugged. What was the use in denying it? "The pool of women in my age range is getting shallow. Especially considering that this city isn't that big. And before you say it, Blue Creek is even smaller, so I'm sure I wouldn't find anyone there, either."

"Don't be so sure about that," Barbara said. "Remember, Tristan just said that new people are moving to Blue Creek all the time."

They got to chatting about lighter topics. He loved hearing about how the Wolfe children … and grandchildren! … were doing and loved, even more, to see how happy Barbara and Tristan were. They'd settled into later life so nicely.

It made him suddenly regret his choice to remain single for so long.

When the check came, he insisted on paying.

They walked out together, and he started to say goodbye when Tristan cleared his throat and looked at Barbara. "It's now or never."

"What?" Rhett asked, suddenly feeling suspicious again.

Barbara pulled her phone out, thumbed over the screen, and then turned it toward him.

"Her name is Sara," Barbara said as Rhett gazed at a photo of the most beautiful woman he'd ever seen. She had a lovely smile, twinkling eyes, and dark curly hair that gave her a playful air.

He couldn't help himself. He took the phone

from Barbara so he could look closer at this woman.

Why did he feel like everything inside him lit up while he looked at her?

Mine. His wolf spoke in a way he'd never heard it before.

He looked back at Barbara and Tristan, bewildered.

They both were looking back at him with knowing grins.

"She'll be at the scenting ceremony at our place next week," Barbara said. "As usual, you're invited to attend."

"I don't know if I can ..." he trailed off. What didn't he know? If he could attend the event? If he could find the nerve to face something he'd avoided for this long in his life ... finding and claiming his mate?

"Well, it's up to you." Barbara shrugged, taking her phone back.

The loss of Sara's photo stung. His empty hand felt much more lonely than before he'd seen her photo.

"The worst that could happen is you check the woman out, don't feel anything, then go home," Barbara continued.

"No, isn't the worst thing if I show up and meet her and realize I can't live my life without her?"

Tristan and Barbara exchanged a loving smile.

"No, my friend," Tristan said, patting him on the shoulder. "That's not the worst thing at all."

CHAPTER THREE

Sara chose a long, flowing maxi dress and a pair of strappy sandals to wear to the scenting ceremony. She left her curly dark hair free to bounce around her face and on her shoulders. She selected a pair of large hoop earrings and several bangle-type bracelets, then she applied a small amount of makeup to take away the appearance of having just crawled out of bed. She completed her look with a nude lip gloss and sighed, knowing this was as good as it was going to get.

Sara arrived at the scenting ceremony, and she could feel the excitement in the air. It reminded her of the many solstice events she'd been a part of in the past, which made her wonder how her new coven celebrated. If they weren't all that fun, then at least she could count on a good time at the Wolfe's, based on what she was seeing so far.

The gathering certainly had that kind of naturalist vibe that Sara liked, with all the torches set up and lanterns hanging from chains that were draped over the tree branches that surrounded the area. While everyone hung out around the Wolfe's home at the moment, she saw the path that went into the field, where an unlit bonfire stood. And then, beyond that, was the forest.

She immediately found Barbara and met her husband, Tristan. But she didn't want to be a bother since, clearly, Barbara had many guests to greet. So Sara walked around the party, introducing herself to people here and there and enjoying the warm welcome everyone gave her.

Then, her eyes landed on a man who piqued her interest.

Damn, he's hot. The man had eyes of a bright icy blue that she could easily get lost in. His jaw had the perfect hard angles that ran to his nice full lips that looked as if they were just waiting to be kissed. Short but messy hair framed his incredibly handsome face. And his smile … it warmed everything inside of her.

The man actually walked over to her.

"Rhett Parker," he said, holding his hand out. His deep timber was like music to her ears. His smile was even more fantastic close-up. Her heart fluttered when Rhett kissed the top of her hand in greeting. For the first time in her life, Sara thought she might swoon. She had no idea that type of charisma was still alive and kicking in the modern male species.

"Oh, hello. I'm Sara." Her voice sounded huskier than it ever had. She had no idea what was up with that. Not wanting to get caught drooling over another woman's man, she quickly asked, "Are you here with your wife?"

He shook his head. "No wife. No girlfriend, either."

"Kids?" I asked, assuming he was here to watch them.

"Nope."

"Oh." Confusion set in. "Are you here to find a mate? I thought this was just for younger wolves mating."

"You say that like you think older wolves might not want mates," he said, though he in no way looked offended.

"I just figured you'd all have found them by

now." Really, she'd kind of started to believe that she was the only mid-lifer still single, but that was silly. Of course, there were plenty of them out in the world … she just hadn't had the pleasure of meeting them.

"The world is a big place, and sometimes we focus on other things than love," Rhett said, his voice almost growling in the sexiest way over the word *love.* "Setting up a business, in my case."

"What do you do for business?" Sara asked, seizing the opportunity to continue the discussion with the hot, available man.

"Home building. Construction," he said, seeming pleased that she cared enough to ask.

Her heart did a strange flutter thing the second he turned that sexy smile on her. She had to admit, he was something else when it came to the looks and charm department. It was almost as if he had been pulled from the pages of one of her steamy romance novels and placed directly in front of her. Maybe she should have put a little more time and effort into her appearance, after all.

"And you? Do you work or partake in hobbies, maybe?" Rhett asked.

"I work," Sara said quickly. "I actually just took

over a bed and breakfast not too far from Blue Creek."

It was the answer she gave non-paranormals, leaving out the part about it being a *for witches* B&B and definitely leaving out the part about her being a mentor for younger witches.

Rhett opened his mouth to comment on that when a petite, very attractive blonde woman who looked to be in her thirties pranced over, putting her hand on Rhett's arm. "I can't believe my eyes. What brings you to this mating ceremony, Rhett? It's been so long."

"It sure has. Have you met Sara?" Rhett smoothly removed the woman's hand from his arm and gestured.

The woman barely spared Sara a glance. "So, what are you doing after the event."

"I think I'll be busy," he replied. Now the woman slowly turned her head toward Sara, looking her up and down with a sneer.

"Well, okay then." The woman shrugged and walked away.

"You have admirers," Sara assessed. "I'm not surprised."

"Oh, Janell is one of those 'just because we're not mates doesn't mean we can't have a good time' girls. I'm sure she's hoping I'm leaving alone at the end of the night and looking for company."

"Oh," Sara said, feeling awkward at having cock blocked him.

"It won't be happening," Rhett said, his eyes smoldering as he took a step closer to her.

Me? Is this guy more interested in me *than a sure thing like Janell?*

It made her stomach jump and her sex heat up. She wanted clarification to make sure her imagination wasn't just assuming things that had no basis in reality. "What won't be? You going home with Janell, or you going home alone?"

"Both."

She gulped.

Rhett seemed unbothered. "So, you run a bed and breakfast. That sounds fun, but what else do you do for fun?"

Sara forced herself to pull it together and participate in the conversation rather than getting swept away in a fantasy about the man standing in front of her. "Hmmm. I like to read and cook. Well, anything in the kitchen, really. I love gardening and being outdoors. The forest is like a second home to me. What about you? What do you like to do for fun?"

She smoothly avoided admitting that the reason she loved the outdoors and woods was because she was a witch. She wasn't sure what Rhett thought about witches, or even if he was a human who didn't know about her kind.

"I can't lie. I'm an outdoorsy kind of guy. There's something about being outside, in nature, that just somehow soothes my soul. I guess it's because no matter where I look, I see the beauty of the world around us … in the trees, colorful flowers, the clouds. All you have to do is just take a look around and let it all sink in. I know it probably sounds cheesy, but nonetheless, it's true."

It didn't sound cheesy. From Rhett, it sounded romantic. Poetic.

"I feel the same way. The only time I don't like to be outside is in the rain or when it's super cold. I really don't find much fun in freezing half to death," she laughed.

"Yeah, I really don't like it when it hurts to breathe because the air is so cold. So I'm with you there. Those days are best spent snuggled up in front of a cozy fire."

"With a good movie," Sara agreed.

"Agreed." They shared another smile, making

Sara feel all sorts of worked up. Was this really happening?

"So, how did you manage to find yourself here tonight, Sara?" Rhett asked.

Hearing her name on his lips sent a tingle from her ears down her neck. It was beautiful.

"I met Barbara at a … thing, … and she invited me." Again, she avoided admitting her witch side. "And you?"

"I grew up here … in this pack," he replied. "But I ended up moving away to a bigger town that had more of a demand for my business."

Her heart sank. Rhett didn't live here, which meant seeing him tonight was probably a one-time thing.

Well, that didn't mean she couldn't enjoy his attentions tonight, right?

CHAPTER FOUR

ine.

Rhett's breath hitched in his throat. Sara was more beautiful than even Barbara's photo had led him to believe. How that was even possible was beyond him. Her dark curls bounced on her shoulders, and she looked delicious in the loose dress she wore. What he wouldn't give for a peek at those beautiful curves of hers.

Her bright emerald eyes lit up when he smiled at her, and everything inside of him yearned to keep her smiling, too. She was beautiful. Absolutely stunning.

Her scent washed over him as they spoke, fogging his brain and drugging his senses. It took all of his willpower … and then some … not to pull her into his arms to see if her bright glossy lips tasted as good as they looked.

He wanted to kiss her more than he wanted his next damn breath. But he feared that one kiss would lead to a touch. A single touch would lead to him stripping her bare and sliding his tongue over every inch of her body.

Besides, that wasn't how a proper gentleman behaved.

His wolf growled in protest. Wasn't that exactly what the scenting ceremony was for? To cast aside proper behavior and to just *feel* for one night? To allow animalistic passion to lead you, rather than ignore it in lieu of human conventions?

Not yet, he told his wolf. *At least let the ceremony officially begin.*

He didn't have to wait long.

A howling sounded, and the crowd … still all in human form … began moving to the clearing in the field, where the bonfire was being lit.

"Oh, is it time?" Sara asked, her eyes showing both curiosity and excitement.

"It is," Rhett replied, offering his arm for her to take so he could escort her.

She hesitated a moment … long enough that it

almost plunged Rhett into despair that his mate wasn't immediately touching him … but she finally placed her hand on his arm.

And his inner wolf howled in approval.

The touch of his mate was glorious.

He placed his free hand over hers as though securing it there. With all the other horny bastards who were here and unable to find a mate but still wanted to get laid, there was no way he was letting her out of his sight tonight.

Or ever, his wolf thought.

She has to have some say in it, Rhett thought to himself. *But we'll do all we can to make sure she chooses me.*

He was certain that Sara wasn't a shifter … he would have smelled her animal if she was … but he also had a feeling that she wasn't simply human, either. What could she be? Not vampire … not unless she was one of the ones who ate grilled chicken and didn't mind daylight … maybe a witch?

He wished he would have asked Barbara before the event. It would have made things a little less awkward.

"So, you've been to one of these before?" Sara asked.

"I have," Rhett said.

He realized that while he knew what was happening, Sara had no idea, so he began explaining it to her.

"Mated couples stay to the back of the crowd, but those who are here hoping to find their mates tonight are at the front, circling the bonfire. This gives them all a chance to look each other over. Usually, a shifter knows from the moment they lay eyes on their mate that they've found them."

"Everyone has been mingling tonight, though," Sara mused. "Doesn't that mean they may have already met?"

"Possibly, though I do know some of the younger ones like to avoid the pre-ceremony mingling just to add a level of surprise and antic-ipation."

"Ah. I see," Sara said as she eyed those nearest to the fire.

"The main couple that will lead off the cere-mony has already met. They already know they're mates, but tonight makes it official."

Sara suddenly looked at him. "Don't you need to get up front there to see if your mate is up there?"

"My mate isn't up there," he replied, his voice

catching on the words *because she's right here, holding my arm.*

He needed to tell her, but he didn't know how.

The crowd began to applaud as the featured couple stepped up to the fire. They were both dressed in robes in the color of their wolves … the man in grey, the woman in a brownish-red.

"Do you know them?" Sara asked.

"I don't." He may know their parents, but from this far away, he didn't know. The pack had grown so much since he'd last lived here that while some faces were familiar, most were new to him.

They watched as the couple touched hands, palms facing each other, as they turned around in a kind of dance. Then, the man walked around the woman. Once he was done, it was her turn.

Then, the kiss.

Rhett heard Sara gasp when the couple embraced, and he couldn't blame her. The passion and tension in the air were palpable.

Then, another howl sounded, and the two shifted into their wolf forms before everyone.

Again, they circled each other, sniffing, and when they were satisfied … or, more specifically, when they could no longer stand to wait … they sprinted off, away from the crowd and into the woods.

The crowd went up in tremendous applause and cheers, while at the same time, all the others hoping to become mated tonight shifted and ran into the woods, going in all different directions.

"They'll meet in wolf form?" Sara asked.

"Some of them, yes," Rhett answered. "They'll shift into human form after that. And if they're agreed, they'll consummate their match out there tonight."

"Sex in the woods," she murmured.

"Does that seem lewd to you?" He hoped not because it sounded very much the opposite to him.

"Oh no." Sara blushed. "I thought it sounded very pleasurable, indeed. As I said, I love the woods."

Good, very good.

Now that the wolves had left, there was more room to get closer to the fire. As they did, Rhett watched in awe as she closed her eyes and let the heat of the flames hit her full force. Only then did he notice the dark red highlights in her hair. They danced in the light breeze, almost as if they had their own agenda.

"Beautiful," he whispered, wanting to reach out

and touch her hair, but he didn't. He kept his one arm still and his other hand firmly holding hers in place.

"What's that?" she asked, turning to face him.

"I was just commenting on the weather. It's turning out to be a beautiful night." The lie burned as it fell from his mouth. Why he felt the need to lie in this situation was beyond him, but he did. Maybe it was because even though every instinct in his body told him to pull her into his arms and kiss the hell out of her, he fought back, not wanting to scare her away.

The *last* thing he wanted was for his mate to have any reason to leave his side right now.

CHAPTER FIVE

He called me beautiful.

She knew he wasn't talking about the weather. She'd caught how he'd been looking at her when he'd said it out of the corner of her eye.

She giggled. A true giddy, schoolgirl giggle. It was the most euphoric feeling passing through her mind and body, both at being called beautiful *and* at the fact that, for some reason, Rhett had felt the need to fib about what he'd said.

He smiled in response to her giggle, and almost started laughing along with her, when he asked, "what's so funny?"

She shook her head. "Nothing."

Not for the first time, she tried to take her hand back from his arm, but again, he held it in place.

Not fiercely enough that she couldn't get away if she wanted to. Just firmly enough to let her know that he didn't want to let her go.

Oh, how that surge of energy had passed right through her fingers and straight to her core the second she'd placed her hand on his arm. It had taken every ounce of her damn willpower not to throw herself into his freaking arms. Right there! Around the bonfire in front of everyone!

That so wasn't her. It had never been. She had always been reserved, and even when she'd had a boyfriend, she had never really participated in public displays of affection. Instead, she only wanted to share those sensual moments in private.

But right now, all those thoughts seemed to go down the drain. She wouldn't have cared less if anyone saw them making out. All she wanted was his lips on hers.

The party had everything she could want. The night air, the big forest nearby, and a very sexy man holding onto her as though she were a life preserver.

She wanted to ask him if they could go for a walk in the woods but wondered if that would be inappropriate if it were off-limits to anyone who wasn't looking for a mate.

But she didn't ask him because she felt it was too risky. If she went into the woods with him, she very well might end up kissing him, letting him hike up her skirt …

Yes, the whole event and being out in nature like this had made her feel friskier than usual.

That, and the fact that Rhett was the hottest man she'd ever seen. She wondered if his lips were as soft as they looked.

"How are you two enjoying the party?"

Sara turned toward the voice and saw Barbara approaching.

Suddenly, she felt like she'd been caught acting like a horny teenager, and she finally pulled her hand away from Rhett.

"It's absolutely lovely," Sara said, hoping Barbara didn't sense how hot she was for this guy.

"I'm glad you're enjoying yourself. And I see you've met Rhett." Barbara raised her eyebrow at him.

"You're right about that," Rhett said. "And about so many other things."

Sara didn't understand what he meant, but

Barbara seemed to. Her face lit up as she exclaimed, "I knew it!"

"Thank you for inviting me," Rhett said, his voice holding a solemn note.

Sara felt like something else was going on between Barbara and Rhett, but she still added her thanks as well. "It's been so nice to be here. Thanks again."

Barbara nodded. Then, her eyes squinted as she looked back and forth between Rhett and Sara.

"What? Do I have something in my teeth?" Sara blurted out the first thought that came to mind, even though that wouldn't explain why Barbara was looking at them *both* oddly.

"No, hon, you look fine," Barbara assured her. "I was just wondering whether or not you two were going to go off into the woods."

Rhett stiffened up beside her, but Sara gasped in excitement. "I would love to walk in the woods. I just didn't know if it was for wolves only."

"Well, Rhett's a wolf," Barbara said. "He can surely escort a witch into the woods."

Sara looked at him hopefully. His face had turned to shock, and Sara didn't know why, so she quickly backpedaled, not wanting to put him out.

"It's okay if you don't want to. I have woods behind my house I can walk in any time. It's fine."

"Oh, trust me, he wants to take you into the woods," Barbara laughed. "But you two should maybe talk a little bit first. Seems I've dropped some information that you two hadn't gotten along to sharing with each other yet."

With that, Barbara moved on, talking to the next group of guests.

"What information?" Sara asked Rhett, and then Barbara's words replayed in her mind. "Oh! That you're a wolf."

"And you're a witch," he said dryly.

"Is that a problem?"

"No," Rhett replied. Then he looked at her curiously. "Why do you sound like you've known people who *did* think that was a problem?"

Sara winced. "I'm not around non-witches very often, and a few times, yeah, I had people ask me to not 'be a witch' around them because my powers made them uncomfortable."

"I hope you told them to fuck off."

Sara laughed. "Yeah, I more or less did. I'm not ever going to apologize for the gifts that I was born with or hide them from the people I consider friends."

She was who the hell she was, and she wasn't about to change for anyone. Lover, friend, or spouse.

Rhett took a breath. "I have no problem with you being a witch, though it would be *easier* if you were a wolf. It's always easier for mates to connect if they both feel the pull. But that doesn't mean it's not possible."

"Mates?" Sara had hardly heard any of his words after that one. "Are you … are you saying I'm your mate?"

He nodded his head gravely. "Leave it to Barbara to make sure the cat got out of the bag quickly."

Her head began to swim, and she had to focus on taking breaths.

"Are you okay?" Rhett asked.

She nodded but suddenly needed to get away from all the other people. "Do you think you'd be up for that walk in the woods?

"Yes, of course."

He offered his hand, and she took it gratefully, feeling herself shaking a bit as she tried to stay calm.

She was Rhett's mate? What did that *really* mean?

She'd never imagined that she might be the mate of a shifter.

As they walked, he asked, "So, you're single. That much I assumed because I didn't figure Barbara would have invited me here to meet you if you were taken."

"Barbara invited you here to meet me?" Sara snapped her eyes toward him, shocked at the revelation.

He looked slightly guilty as he admitted, "I believe Barbara pegged you as my mate the moment she met you. She has a gift for this kind of thing. She and Tristan made the trip out to have dinner with me a week ago, to show me your picture and tell me to get my ass out here to meet you."

"Oh." Sara felt in shock.

They'd crossed the tree line, and though she knew that the other wolves were somewhere in the forest, they still felt completely alone.

Rhett stopped walking to turn and face her, taking her free hand in his so he was holding both of hers. "And I'm *so very* grateful that she did. I hope you are, too."

Dumbfounded, Sara nodded. "I am."

"Good," Rhett said, letting go of one of her

hands to push back some of her wild hair. "Now, there's something I've been wanting to do since the moment I saw you."

"What's that?" she asked in a breathy voice.

"This," he whispered as his lips closed gently over hers.

His kiss was completely unexpected. It made her head spin. His lips were just as soft and warm as she'd thought they would be, and a small moan escaped her. He quickly took advantage of the opening and slid his tongue into her mouth. His exploration was gentle and sweet while his arms wrapped around her in a firm embrace. He pulled her closer until her body was flush against his.

Her arms wound around his neck, almost as if it were an automatic response to his closeness. She had been dying for a kiss since their first meeting, and she was finally getting it. It was more than she could have ever expected.

The heat from his body scorched every inch of hers and traveled directly to her core, igniting every primal womanly need inside of her.

CHAPTER SIX

After all these years, Rhett had finally found his mate.

Every word Sara said in her sweet voice had been like music to his ears. He swore that his heart skipped a beat or two every time she smiled. And that smile of hers, well, it made him want to kiss her until she moaned his name and begged for more.

He was a goner, and he knew it. There was no denying that he was already head over heels for the woman he had just met … his mate. And it was all thanks to Barbara.

Over the years, he had often wondered if the whole fated mate thing was nothing but a myth, but he saw Barbara and Tristan together and couldn't deny their relationship had to have indeed been a blessing from the fates. He'd just never thought he could feel that way himself.

Yet, here he was, kissing his mate and feeling more alive than he'd ever felt in his entire life.

More alive than he could have possibly imagined.

They finally broke apart, only to catch their breath. The passion that existed between them had certainly stolen that breath away from both of them.

They stood there, panting in the woods, the only illumination coming from the moonlight that filtered down through the tree canopy.

He wanted to drag her off the path they were standing on. Wanted to find a secluded space so he could fully have her, but reason prevailed. He couldn't rush her into something she wasn't ready for. He needed to be sure she was okay with this first.

"So, you never said what you thought about being my mate," he said, needing to hear her put words to what she was feeling. It was obvious that lust simmered within her for him, but when he informed her that she was his mate, she was obviously shocked.

At least she hadn't been shocked enough to run away.

She didn't answer him. Instead, she started walking further into the forest. He didn't move for a moment. Instead, he admired the view.

The sway of her hips. Her perfect ass.

His cock was rock hard and begging for attention. Her scent lingered on his skin and in his nostrils, driving him wild and making him want her more than his next breath.

"So, do you want to go first, or do you want me to go first?" she asked.

He blinked at her in confusion. He'd asked her what she thought about being his mate, and this wasn't an answer.

"I want to see your wolf, and I'm guessing you want to see my magic," she clarified. "So, who's first?"

Okay. Sure, he could do that. Whatever he needed to do to make her feel better.

"I can show you mine first if it will help make you feel more comfortable."

She nodded. He stepped off the path, trekking a bit through the trees before he stripped out of his clothes. Then, Rhett drew in a deep breath and called on the magic he had been born with. Immediately he felt a drop in the atmospheric pressure. The wind picked up and swirled around him. Each bone in his body snapped and began to transform. His face elongated, and fur sprouted across his body. Within seconds, he stood on four feet instead of two.

He heard Sara gasp and watched as her face contorted with shock. He calmly sat on his hind legs and let her get used to the idea that he had just shifted into a wolf. What he wouldn't give to have their mate link activated already, so they could speak telepathically. He would love to know exactly what it was that was running through that beautiful head of hers.

SARA COULD HARDLY BELIEVE IT, and in fact, she wouldn't believe it at all if she hadn't just watched as the most handsome man she had ever met turned into the most beautiful black wolf she had ever laid her eyes on.

Sure, she'd just seen a whole pack of young wolves change and run into the woods, but there was something different about watching it so close-up, and to someone you'd been feeling attraction to … someone she'd just been kissing!

Plus, Rhett's wolf was huge! Nearly half the size of a horse! She had no idea wolves could be so damn big. And his eyes … they were still his. Yes, those mesmerizing eyes of his were blessedly the same.

She wanted to pet him to see if his fur was as soft and thick as it looked, but she had no idea if he was in full control of himself or not. It certainly seemed like he was, especially when he sat back on his haunches and whined at her. Would it be safe to approach him and pet him?

One of the memes she had shared on Facebook popped into her mind: *I will most likely die petting something I shouldn't!*

She laughed at the thought of the funny meme.

"Can you understand me?" she asked, wondering how much of Rhett was truly present when he was in his wolf form.

The wolf nodded at her.

"Well, how about that. I just want to pet you. Is that a bad thing?" she asked.

He whined again and shook his head back and forth. Then, he stood and slowly began to walk forward, his tail slowly swishing behind him in a happy way with each step.

Sara crouched down as Rhett inched closer to her.

Rhett came to a stop and sat in front of her, placing his snout on her knee.

Surprised by the action, Sara giggled and scratched behind his ears. "Aren't you a good boy?"

A low rumble left his mouth.

"Sorry, sorry. I just couldn't resist. You *are* a handsome wolf, though," she said, slowly running her fingers over the top of his head and down his neck. "Your fur is so soft."

Rhett wiggled a little closer, his nose inching toward her core.

"Hey! We'll have none of that," she laughed, pushing his big head away from her. Before she could protest further, he walked around her, sniffing her legs and even her ass before she swatted him away.

He continued his circle and then stopped in front of her, staring hard at her for a moment before he turned away and shifted back into his human form.

She waited for him to dress and turn back to face her.

"Now, it's your turn," he said with an expectant look.

"I suppose you're right. Though, I'm not sure I can top that. I definitely don't shift into a cool animal like you do. I just hope what I have to show you, well … I hope it doesn't make me look stupid compared to *your* brand of paranormal."

Suddenly, Sara wasn't afraid of showing him that she was a witch. She was just hoping that he wasn't expecting her to transform into something amazing like he did. Because if that was the case, he was about to be seriously disappointed.

"There's nothing you can do that will make you look stupid. That I can promise you."

"If you say so." He was nice to say that, but she wasn't sure that she believed him.

"I'm serious, Sara. I can't imagine there is anything that you could do that would be a turn-off … or make you look stupid."

She turned and smiled at him, feeling the sincerity and truth in his words. He had meant every word that he had said. Of that, she was one-hundred percent certain.

"Okay. Here goes nothing." Sara bent down and plucked a small handful of dandelions from the grass. She whispered a few words under her breath, then blew on the seed heads. As they floated away on her breath, each head began to glow as they broke apart and floated into the air until they paused just above their heads and formed a bright white heart before changing colors to a soft red, blue, and finally, purple. Sara let go of her magic hold on the seeds and allowed them to continue on their journey when a light breeze picked up.

"Okay, that was pretty freaking awesome," Rhett said with a smile.

"Yeah, it was. Wasn't it?" The fact was that Sara loved her magic. She always had. It was fun to practice and even more fun when she got to show off her skills just a bit. Especially when she was able to come up with cool spells like the one she had just shown Rhett.

"Can you do that again?" he asked, inching closer to where she stood.

"Sure," she laughed and reached down to grab another handful of dandelions. "I've always had a thing for these flowers. I always thought they were pretty … even if most people consider them a weed."

"I think I'll always have a soft spot for them now," he replied.

She blushed, and her heart swelled. "Okay, let's do a different shape this time."

"I don't mind a heart. I liked it."

"Another heart it is then."

Sara whispered the same chant and blew out a breath, scattering the seed heads once again. They repeated the same path as the previous ones. She turned to face Rhett to see what he thought about the repeated spell. He wasn't watching the seed heads float away. His eyes were trained on every move she made.

"Is everything…"

His mouth closed over hers, and she gasped in surprise. The kiss that he had given her just a moment ago had been gentle and sweet. This kiss was not that. It was anything but sweet and gentle.

CHAPTER SEVEN

"Goodness," Sara whispered, pulling back from the hotter-than-hell kiss for a brief second before diving back in for more.

The tender, exploratory kiss he had given her when they first stepped into the woods was nothing like this. Now, he kissed her with a need and desire deeper than the ocean and hotter than hell. His heat shot through her body and straight to her core and sent moan after moan from her lips to his.

He laid her down on the ground, and she wrapped her arm around his neck and pulled him as close as she possibly could, wanting more of his heat. His hands roamed freely over her body, coming to a stop at her breasts. He caressed and massaged them before tweaking her already hardened nipples with his thumbs.

She tossed her head back and glanced up at the trees as he kissed a path down her neck and between the valley of her breasts.

"Oh, Rhett!" she moaned.

"You taste so damn good. I want more," he groaned. "I *need* more."

"So do I!" she gasped, pulling him on top of her. She pushed against him, rubbing against his jeans in a frantic gyration for release. "Get your fucking pants off."

He growled but didn't do as she ordered. Instead, he continued worshiping her body. Each new kiss of his was needier than the previous one, which suited Sara just fine. The anticipation of release was delicious.

Her hormones were running on overdrive, and Rhett was egging them on with every single touch of his. Not that she minded. She loved every single kiss, every single brush of his skin against hers. It was like every nerve ending in her body ignited at once, sending her into a lust-fueled frenzy of want and need.

"You taste so fucking good. I wanna' strip you

bare. I want your sweetness all over my tongue and running down my throat," Rhett groaned, his hands working up her thighs underneath her dress.

Sara was starting to wonder if she could climax just from Rhett kissing her and touching her skin. It had been so damn long.

The thought had her freezing. What was she doing?

"Are you okay?" Rhett asked.

"Yeah," Sara sighed. "I just … I'm not sure … should we be doing this?"

"If you want to stop, we'll stop," Rhett said, pulling his tight black t-shirt over his head, only to display row after row of rippling muscles. "Just say the word."

"Oh, well, that's just not fair." Sara sucked in a sharp breath and felt all her doubts melting away. Who said that just because she was in mid-life that she couldn't get down and dirty in the woods with a man who was as ripped as Tarzan? She wanted to run her tongue over every one of those beautiful muscles of his and the few tattoos that were perfectly placed on his chest, back, and arms.

"Do you want to stop?" Rhett asked. "Or can I taste you?"

His fingers gently grazed her panty line between her legs. The material was already soaked, that much she was sure of.

"Yes," Sara whispered, her entire body shaking with need. There was no denying how badly she wanted him, even though there were several fears ravaging her brain. All the reasons she should say no seemed to pop into her mind at the exact same time, but she pushed them back. Every single one of those little bitches. She was a grown-ass woman, and he was a grown-ass man. There wasn't a single damn reason, good reason, for her to tell him no. Not when every inch of her body screamed at her to say yes. So, that was exactly what she had done.

He only growled his response before dipping his fingers under the material to slide through her wet sex. Then, he pulled them away and licked her juices.

She would probably spontaneously combust if she was denied any sort of climax at this point. Her body would fall into a revolt when it came to that nonsense, and rightfully so. But she didn't have to worry about that. He looked like a man savoring a delicacy before he went back in, quickly ripping the panties off her body and then diving his face into her pussy.

She hiked her dress up above her hips, so she could watch his head bob as he licked and suckled her, drawing out cries as her body tingled in pleasure.

"Oh, Rhett!" Sara moaned as he slid his tongue over her folds. Her limbs trembled. She tossed her head back and forth, knowing she was going to end up with all sorts of dirt, twigs, and leaves in her hair but not caring one bit.

She reached down to touch his hair as he lifted her legs over his shoulders.

"I swear, this is the sweetest damn honey I've ever tasted," Rhett groaned. "I could do this all day, every day, and never tire of it."

"Oh, yes! Don't stop!" Sara shouted as he pushed one and then two fingers deep inside of her while his tongue focused on her clit, driving her to the brink of madness.

"Rhett! I'm going to come!" Sara shouted, her hand blindly reaching for him until his free hand grasped it, giving her something solid to hold onto while her body soared out into oblivion.

"That's it, Sara. Let go. I've got you. I want to

taste your sweet juices. I want it running down my throat."

"Yes! Yes!" She rocked her hips back and forth as her climax crashed over her and pulled her into an unknown universe. The force of the orgasm rocked her to the very core, cracking open something inside of her she hadn't even known existed.

They were just on the oral part of the evening, and she had already had the most powerful orgasm in her damn life.

She distantly felt the scratch of his lips over hers once more and his hands making quick work of sliding her maxi dress off of her while her body shook as she came down from her climax.

"You are so damn beautiful," Rhett growled. "Especially when you come. I love your taste. I love watching you succumb to pleasure. I've never seen anything hotter in my life."

Sara watched him sit back in the moonlight. When had he gotten rid of his pants? She didn't know, but there he was, as nude as she was, while he palmed his cock. He stroked it up and down, nice and slow, teasing her with his motions.

"I want to feel you inside of me," Sara moaned. Her hand slipped down her body to the juncture between her thighs. She was still sensitive from her orgasm, but drawing long lines through her moisture was enough to tease him back.

"Is that so?" Rhett asked, positioning himself between her legs.

"Mmmhmm," she moaned as he pressed the head of his cock against her entrance.

"I want you, too," he said, slowly inching into her.

She gasped, and he leaned down, pressing his mouth against hers, kissing her while he slid fully inside of her.

***

RHETT BIT the inside of his cheek. The urge to come within the first few seconds of being inside of Sara rode him harder than he could have ever imagined. She was so fucking tight, hot, and wet. She fit him like a damn glove. It was the sweetest, most perfect combination of the perfect woman.

"Fuck," he groaned as he shifted his hips and pulled out to the tip before sinking back into her.

"Sex has never felt this damn good," she groaned, bringing a smile to his face.

He didn't know why a single statement brought such joy to him, but it did. Stretching his lean muscles over her body, he pushed her arms above her head and held them there as he started a series of long, lazy strokes into Sara's heat.

He kissed and licked and nibbled on every inch of her soft skin. When it came down to it, there wasn't a single part of his mate's body that he planned on leaving untouched in some shape or form. Whether he kissed and licked or touched and massaged, he would have her begging for more. He would make her come to realize that he was the only one who could work her body into a frenzy and give her what she truly needed and wanted.

It was a tall order to fill, but he was up for the challenge. She was his mate, and he would do whatever it took to give her the pleasure she deserved. What he was about to unleash on his unsuspecting mate was nothing short of owning every inch of her body with his.

He wanted her legs shaking, her breaths uneven, her head ready to pop off her shoulders, and he wanted her screaming his damn name over and over until she related his name with the purest of raw fucking pleasure.

He hitched her legs over his shoulders, pulling out to the tip before slamming back inside of her.

Leaves flew up from the ground around them after the sheer force of his thrust. Those beautiful full tits of hers bounced back and forth and side to side. Skin slapped against skin as he began pounding her in a lust-fueled frenzy that had Rhett ready to lose his damn mind.

"Rhett! Rhett! Oh!" Sara shouted, tossing her head back and forth.

"Oh, God! I can feel you coming all over my cock. So fucking hot. So damn good."

"Whatever you do, don't stop! Please, God, don't you dare stop!" Sara begged as her climax dragged her into oblivion.

"I wouldn't dare stop. As far as I'm concerned, we're just getting started," he growled, twisting his hips and pistoning in and out of her tight sheath.

"Yes! Yes! Yes!" Sara chanted as one release quickly turned into two.

Rhett loved how her pussy squeezed him tight and tried to milk his seed out of him, but he wouldn't give it up. Not yet. Not until Sara was ready to pass out and couldn't take so much as another inch of his dick.

"I want you on your knees," Rhett said, releasing her legs from around his neck.

"Oh, God! Yes! I need to feel you like that," Sara

said, quickly getting on our hands and knees as he had asked.

Seeing her in the moonlight, on her knees with her legs spread, waiting for his cock was almost Rhett's undoing. She looked so fucking hot. The image would be ingrained in his mind for eternity. Wrapping his palm around his cock, he slid the tip over her clit and up to her soaked channel, teasing her for a brief second before thrusting balls deep in one swift move.

"Fuck!" he groaned.

"Rhett! Oh!" she shouted at the sudden but welcomed intrusion.

His fingers tunneled through her hair as he set off on a wicked pace of slamming in and out of her. Sweat beaded over his brow and down his face, but that didn't slow him down. Not for a second. He let go of her hair and grabbed onto her hips. It was a punishing grip. He held her tight as his cock pummeled in and out of her.

He fought back every instinct in his mind and in his body that screamed for him to claim his mate. His wolf tried to force control and take what was his, but Rhett denied the beast within. That simple denial sparked fury within him. His dual nature had always been in sync. By denying his animal's base need and raw instinct, he had inadvertently set off a chain of events that he had no way of stopping.

This is what we're here for. This is what the scenting ceremony is for: to claim our mate, his wolf shouted.

He couldn't hold off any longer. Her body brought him too much pleasure. As he reached his climax, Rhett bit down on Sara's shoulder.

The mark he was leaving on her body was the official claiming, and along with the seed he spilled inside her now, it would bind them together, telling all other shifters that Sara was *his*.

CHAPTER EIGHT

Sara's body quaked as she came down from her final climax. Every inch of her body was hyper-sensitive to the smallest of touches. Each brush of his fingers over her skin sent new surges of pleasure shooting through her. She had never felt anything like it in her entire life.

Rhett kissed and licked her full breasts as she ran her fingers through his thick dark hair. "Mmmm," she softly moaned. "That was amazing."

"Better than I could have imagined," Rhett said, rolling to his side.

The two of them laying there, naked on the forest floor, brought a sense of peace to her that she wasn't sure could ever be replicated.

They were in the absolute most perfect moment that she could ever imagine.

The smile on his face melted her heart. And good God, those eyes of his, reflecting the moonlight as he gazed at her. She melted even further into them. How that was even possible was beyond her, but she did.

As her senses returned, she felt an aching pain on her shoulder. She reached up and touched the spot. It was wet.

She looked at her fingers and saw the blood on them.

She looked at Rhett questioningly. Had he bitten her? She didn't remember it, but she'd been far too lost in the heat of the moment to process everything that was happening at once.

The entire experience was like nothing she could have ever dreamed possible. Especially this late in life. Sara thought for certain that there was nothing new she could learn or discover when it came to sex.

Boy, was she wrong. Seriously fucking wrong.

He pressed his lips together. "Yeah, about that. We should probably talk about it," Rhett said, sitting up.

An uneasy feeling settled in the pit of Sara's

stomach at the sudden serious look on Rhett's face. The post-coital bliss she had been feeling vanished instantly. "What's wrong?"

"It occurs to me that perhaps you weren't fully aware what you were walking into tonight and that my animal side may have …"

"May have *what?*" Sara asked, sitting up and finding her clothes to dress as he'd started to do the same.

She touched the wound again and noticed it was healing already.

"I marked you."

"Marked me?"

"Claimed," he added. "As my official mate."

She blinked at him. "Um, isn't that something maybe I should have had a say in?"

He nodded, looking properly chagrined. "I'm sorry. I got caught up in the moment. In the night. In the excitement of meeting you and in the knowledge that tonight is a special night for mates. The night we're *supposed* to claim our mates."

Sara was at a loss. "What exactly does this mean for *me?*"

"You'll have a scar there, for one."

"And for two?"

"Other shifters will know you've been claimed.

You may find that other shifters won't want to date you."

What? Sara took a deep breath. She was having a hard time processing what had just happened and what it all meant, and she didn't think she was going to get any clarity on it all standing there in the woods.

"I need to go home." She started walking back toward the path.

"Sara. Please," Rhett begged, reaching out to stop her, but she avoided his grasp.

"No." Sara felt her magic bubbling just under her skin, but it was more than that. There was something else driving her anger. She just couldn't put her finger on what it was. Her magic felt somehow different. Like she was more powerful somehow. Was it because the anger was fueling it?

Sara refused to so much as glance back at Rhett, though she heard his steps behind her as she marched out of the woods, through the field, and around the house to her car.

She slammed her car door and locked it. She saw Rhett's figure, standing off in the distance, near the house. She shook her head in disgust as she pulled away from the Wolfe's place.

Nothing about this evening had gone the way

that Sara had hoped or expected. Meeting Rhett had been great, and so was the little magic show they both had performed. Even the sex was mind-blowingly fantastic. Right up until the end when Rhett had to go and fuck it all up by marking her as his mate without even so much as a single conversation regarding the subject.

That was what had pissed her off the most. She might have understood if he would have said, *hey, if we have sex out here in the woods during the scenting ceremony, I'm going to have a hard time holding myself back from marking you.*

She wondered what she would have said if he *had* let her know that was a possibility. Part of her thought that she was so caught up in the night's excitement that she probably would have told him, *go ahead.*

There was a magic in the air, she knew that much, and sometimes you couldn't resist when magic pushed.

He had been swept up in things more powerful than they were. Fate, magic, ceremony … it all added up to what had happened between them … from the fantastic sex to the mating bite. Rhett wouldn't have ever been in this position before. Shifters usually only get one mate, so that would mean that Sara was the first woman he'd connected with at a scenting ceremony.

How was he supposed to know he'd lose control and bite her?

It was unreasonable for her to expect him to have given her a warning. She understood getting swept away by magic.

As she left the Blue Creek town line, she couldn't deny that she was less mad at Rhett for losing control and more terrified of what this actually meant for her.

I've been outside the Academy for such a short time, and suddenly I'm mated to a wolf? What does that mean for me?

She needed some sleep. Some time to clear her head.

She almost decided to hop into bed as soon as she arrived home, but despite the fact that it was nearly two in the morning, she needed to clean up first. She was filthy from the forest floor.

Plus, she wanted to wash away the feeling of Rhett.

As the warm water washed over her, she honed in on that idea. She needed to just forget about him. Forget that he'd marked her. *She* wasn't a shifter, so what difference did it make to her life if she had some stupid scar on her shoulder?

So it might make her undesirable to other shifters. Oh well. She could date another witch. Or a vampire. Or heck, even a regular old human.

Or she could just go back to living her life the way she had for so many years already: alone. Doing her own thing without having anyone else messing things up for her.

Easier said than done. She pulled the twigs and leaves out of her hair, and her mind flashed back to the sex they'd had, and immediately her core heated.

Her body still wanted him, even if her mind was trying to forget him.

That much was made even more clear when she soaped up her loofah and rubbed it over her body. Her nipples, in particular, perked right up, giving her thoughts of his hands and mouth on them.

She tried to push the thoughts of him out of her mind, but as she closed her eyes and relaxed into the water, she realized that something inside her body felt different. Yes, the sexual awareness was there, but something else was too.

Did this have something to do with the mating bite?

She sighed as she left the shower. Maybe it was just the post-sex high. Perhaps she'd wake up feeling like herself again.

If not, she would need to call up Barbara and get the full details on what this claiming bite meant.

CHAPTER NINE

The next afternoon, Sara forced herself to leave her bed after sleeping nearly twelve hours. She yawned as she waited for her pot of coffee to finish. One of these days, she swore that she was going to invest in one of those single-cup coffee makers … even if she did still end up making a whole pot of coffee a damn cup at a time. It had to be faster than waiting for the entire pot.

She yawned again, feeling like she could crawl back into bed and sleep away the rest of the day. She couldn't remember a time in her life before this when she'd slept so much, but she'd also never had wild sex in the woods with multiple orgasms for hours before either.

As soon as the coffee finished brewing, Sara poured herself a cup and added her cream and sugar. Grabbing her tablet, she padded to her screened-in porch and relished the beautiful afternoon sunshine.

She was doing everything she could to not think about Rhett, but she couldn't help but be surprised that she hadn't heard from him. He hadn't texted or shown up, pounding her door down, demanding to speak with her.

Sure, they hadn't exchanged numbers or addresses, but she figured Rhett would try to get that info from Barbara. Maybe Barbara respected a woman's right to turn a man down.

It still infuriated her that she bore a scar on her shoulder that she hadn't asked for and that it somehow marked her as 'off limits' to other shifters. No, she wouldn't accept that. She hadn't ever let other people make decisions for her. Not in her younger years, and she surely would not start now.

Taking a few sips of her coffee, she let the caffeine kick in before opening up emails and then reading over the morning news. The news was too depressing to read, so she closed out of it.

A notification popped up. It was from Bryce, the man she'd been talking to on the dating app.

She hesitated. Her finger hovered over the notification.

Should she talk to him still? When she belonged to Rhett?

Screw that! She decided. Rhett might have marked her, but that doesn't mean she can't still live her life how she wanted to. She had known Rhett for one night. Sure, they'd had great sex, and maybe if he hadn't ruined things by biting her, then maybe they would have developed a relationship.

But as it was, she had no desire to see him, so why not talk to Bryce?

Because Bryce has nothing on Rhett. After such a night of passion with Rhett, I'd be slumming it with anyone else.

Well, that's exactly what rebounds were, right? A way to kiss a frog to forget the prince, because this one might not work out, but then at least the next one won't seem so bad.

She looked at the message from Bryce:

So, dinner tonight?

That's right. She'd forgotten that he'd asked,

and she'd told him that it depended on how she felt after the event she had to go to the night before.

Again, she felt no desire to say yes, but she knew she had to get out of her house.

So, she agreed.

She didn't want to go off on a date without letting anyone know where she was, and she didn't want to put that kind of stress on her apprentice, so she called the one person she thought would be okay with it.

"Sara, how are you?" Barbara asked when she answered the phone.

"Fine," Sara sighed.

"Rhett didn't tell me what went so badly between you two, but he was pretty insistent when trying to get me to give over your number."

"But you said no." A statement, not a question. No way she wouldn't have heard from Rhett if he'd been successful in his efforts.

"I did," Barbara confirmed. "But I told him that if you called and said it was okay, I'd hand it over. *Is* that why you're calling."

"No," Sara said, holding her ground. "I actually wondered if you could do me a favor."

She explained the date with Bryce and her desire for someone to know where she was.

There was a momentary silence, and Sara was sure Barbara wanted to ask her about Rhett, but instead, the woman simply said, "Of course. And if you want to text me an SOS to get you out of there, feel free. I'll call you and tell you there's an emergency thing I need your help with."

Sara chuckled. "I knew I could count on you."

Sara thanked her and started to say goodbye, but Barbara stopped her.

"I know you'd probably prefer for me to stay out of it, but I'd be a bad friend to Rhett if I didn't tell you that he's a really good guy. Whatever he said or did that upset you so much, I'm sure …"

"Don't say he didn't mean it," Sara said. "And don't say he regrets it because he doesn't. And I can't deal with him. So I'm going out on this date to try to shake Rhett out of my system and move on."

"Mates don't get over it that easy," Barbara said softly.

"Witches don't have mates," Sara retorted.

"Fair enough. Well, I hope you have a nice date tonight."

"Thank you." Sara hung up the phone, trying not to be affected by Barbara's words.

She hadn't known the woman long, but she

liked Barbara. Trusted her. So Barbara's words about Rhett meant something to her.

She had to shake it off. She had a date to get ready for.

Why was she nervous? It was just dinner, right? How bad could it be?

That was a question that Sara decided she would never ask again.

After being a nervous wreck about her date all day, she finally pushed through the crippling anxiety and forced herself to get it together and get ready for her dinner date.

When she pulled up to the restaurant, she popped open the visor mirror and checked her hair and makeup one last time, wanting to make a good impression.

She sucked in a deep breath and exited her car, heading for the front door of the restaurant. Her nerves were frazzled, but a nice glass of wine or two would help that issue.

To her surprise, Bryce met her at the bar and greeted her with a hug and a peck on the side of her cheek.

"You look lovely," he said, pulling back from the hug and hesitating with his hand on her arm, looking at her a bit curiously.

"Thank you," Sara replied. Feeling paranoid, she realized that his hand was resting close to the shoulder that Bryce had marked. It had to be a coincidence, right? "Is anything wrong?"

"No, not at all." He seemed to shake it off and grinned widely, guiding her to a quiet booth near the rear of the room. "I took the liberty of ordering your favorite wine." He motioned for the waiter to fill their glasses.

"How did you know?" Sara asked.

"It was on your profile." He smiled at her.

"Oh, that's right. Sorry," she apologized, feeling quite out of sorts. She sipped at her wine and gathered her bearings, trying to figure out what it was about the man in front of her that didn't feel right.

It couldn't *just* be that he wasn't Rhett, right? She refused to believe that the wolf shifter had ruined her for every other man.

On the surface, he was handsome and looked just like his picture, but there was something that didn't jive with his profile description. Was it his age? It had been listed as fifty on the dating site, and while she knew that some men aged like fine wine, she doubted anyone could age *that* well. Sure, Bryce had some grey in his hair, but his face was wrinkle-free and not in the Botox way. He didn't seem to have a single laugh line or wrinkle anywhere on his face or on the back of his hands.

There was something in his body language, too. Or maybe she was just comparing him to Rhett, who had charisma, confidence, and grace in spades. Bryce, on the other hand, just seemed … boyish.

They were supposedly the same age, or so his profile had said. But sitting across from him, she found that hard to believe. She had been around many men her age, and there was a fundamental difference between people her age and someone significantly younger.

Looking closer, she thought the streaks of gray through his hair looked almost intentional … like he'd had highlights, or in this case, gray lights. It was quite perplexing.

During the course of dinner, Sara also noticed several other things that just didn't fit with his listed age, and not that she had been purposely stereotyping him or anything like that. He didn't speak like he was someone in the throes of mid-life, but that of someone much, much younger.

"Is there something wrong?" he asked, probably because she was staring at him, trying to piece together the puzzle.

"I'm just trying to figure you out," she said flatly. Sara wanted all the cards on the table. She usually had some pretty good intuition about people, and it bothered her that she couldn't figure out if there was something off about Bryce or if she was simply so hung up on Rhett that this other man seemed inferior in comparison.

"Ask away. I'm an open book." Bryce threw his arms open, indicating that she should ask away.

"How old are you?" she asked, wanting to see if he would double down on the age listed on his profile.

As soon as the question registered in his brain, a look of shock crossed his handsome wrinkle-free face.

"What makes you think it's different from what I stated on my profile?" he tried and failed to school his annoyance at her question.

"The lack of wrinkles on your hands and face. Also, honestly, the lack of life experience that was painfully present during our conversation. I liked you, Bryce. You seem nice enough, but something is off. What I can't figure out is why you'd lie about your age. Most people always knock a few years off. Hell, I considered it. People don't usually add years to their age. So, I'm trying to figure out why a handsome guy, such as yourself, would do that … on purpose." She motioned for the waiter to refill her glass.

Bryce set his napkin beside his plate and leaned back in his seat. "I'm surprised you picked up on it so easily. Most women don't notice."

Sara shrugged, feeling much bolder than usual for some reason. "It's pretty obvious to anyone who pays attention to the person they are with, or I guess you could sum it up to me not being like most women." And she wasn't. She wasn't just a run-of-the-mill human woman. She was a witch and a powerful one at that.

"Maybe it's because most women are so hung up on talking about themselves, they don't really pay attention," Bryce said.

"That could be, but it still doesn't explain why you do it." She countered.

"There are a couple of reasons. For one, I like older women. There's nothing hotter than a woman who knows who she is and what she wants," he explained, suddenly looking excited.

"That can't be the only reason for the elaborate ruse. Surely, it's not just to lure women to your bed," she laughed at the mere thought.

"While it is a leading factor, no. It's not the only

reason. Older men tend to get more respect than someone my age. They get better job offers and better pay. So, I figured why not? Why should I be discriminated against because I'm younger than my colleagues?"

"Wow." Sara didn't know how to respond to the cocky little sucker sitting in front of her. "So, how old *are* you?" she asked cautiously.

"I'll be twenty-five next month."

"Oh, no," she gasped. "I'm old enough to be your mom!"

"It's not like that. You are hot for your age, and trust me when I tell you there are things I could do to you that would make you forget about the age difference," he said proudly.

"Okay, I think we're done here."

"Oh, come on now. It's not like I'm the only one who lies. You listed on your profile that you were never married!"

"I'm not married!" She objected. "Never have been!"

He rolled his eyes. "Semantics. Mated is the same as married in the shifter world. So, what's going on here? You stepping out on your man, or you a widow, or what?"

Sara's mouth dropped open in shock. So Bryce

was a shifter, and Rhett's mark had been somehow noticeable to him.

She wasn't going to ask him how he'd noticed it. She didn't want to reveal that she knew nothing about the mark she bore on her shoulder.

She shook her head and motioned for the waiter, asking for the check as soon as he approached.

"Really?" Bryce balked. "Just like that? You don't want to explore the options here? I don't need some commitment. I'm happy to fuck your brains out if the man at home is failing to perform."

"He is *not* failing to perform," Sara snapped, coming to Rhett's defense though she had no idea why she felt the urge to.

Her tone clearly irritated Bryce. He sat back in his seat with a sneer on his face. "So maybe you're just such an uptight bitch that he wants nothing to do with your frigid pussy." He snatched the bill out of her hands and threw some bills in the folder. "I pay my own way," he growled before storming out of the restaurant.

Sara laughed at the situation. What the hell was she supposed to say? It was the second night in a row that she ended up going home alone and annoyed.

Getting back into the field of dating wasn't going as she had expected.

CHAPTER TEN

Sara called Barbara as she drove home, using her car's hands-free Bluetooth mode.

"How did your date go?" Barbara asked as soon as she answered. No, *hello, how are you?* Nothing like that. Just straight to the point.

Sara groaned.

"That bad?" Barbara asked.

"Girl. He lied about his age so he could hook up with older women and get respect and promotions easier at work."

"You're kidding!" Barbara sounded just as shocked as Sara had been when the words left Bryce's mouth.

"I wish! It turned into a complete disaster. When I called him out on it, he stormed out of the restaurant." The scene replayed in Sara's mind, and yet, all she could do was laugh. It wasn't like she'd formed a connection or bond or anything. Reluctantly, she added, "and that was after he accused me of being mated already."

"He was a shifter?" Barbara asked before gasping. "Wait, why would he accuse you of being mated already?"

"Actually, that's what I called to ask you about," Sara sighed. "How does one shifter know if someone has already been claimed."

"It's a scent thing," Barbara explained. "When a proper claiming takes place, something happens between the participants that inherently changes their natural scent."

"So it's basically like a dog peeing on a building?"

"That's not exactly how I'd talk about it," Barbara replied. "We usually talk about it in a more sacred and romantic way."

Sara rubbed her temples, feeling a headache come on.

"Hon, why are you asking this?" Barbara asked though she sounded like she already had a good idea why.

"He bit me," Sara said. "We had sex in the woods, and he bit me. Rhett, that is, not Bryce."

Barbara was silent for a moment. Too silent.

"What?" Sara asked. "What are you thinking?"

"I'm thinking that you mated with a wolf yesterday and then went out with a different shifter today. That's quite a complicated scenario. One that could end up with two pissed-off males fighting over you."

"Why?" Sara couldn't keep the annoyance out of her voice. "I didn't ask to be mated. I shouldn't have my life dictated by some action that some out-of-control wolf did while we had sex."

With that, Barbara gasped. "You said he bit you. I didn't realize you weren't consulted beforehand."

"Well, then you can appreciate why I have no desire to talk to Rhett."

"Yes, I can." After another beat of silence, Barbara added, "I am so sorry this has happened. I can't imagine that type of decision being made for me. The whole point of a mating is for it to be a special bond between the couple where they both know what's going on. Please call me whenever you need to talk, okay? I'm here to help."

"I appreciate the offer. Okay, I'm just pulling

into the driveway. I'm going to go so I can get this damn bra off. I can't believe I got all dressed up for that little puke. Talk about a complete waste of make-up. Sheesh."

The first thing she did when she walked through the door was yank the bra off from under her dress. "I'm not sad to see you go," she said, breathing a sigh of relief. Quickly changing into a pair of yoga pants and a tank top, she pulled her hair up and clicked on the TV … the house was far too quiet for her liking.

What now?

Two nights in a row dealing with infuriating men left Sara feeling a deep desire to do *something* in retaliation.

Grabbing her tablet and another glass of wine, she opened up the dating app and navigated to Bryce's profile, looking for the 'unlike' button.

"There should be a dislike or *strongly dislike* button," Sara muttered. "A way to downvote the fucker for all his lies and terrible attitude."

Of course, there was nothing like that available to sate her desire for revenge.

"Okay, how about a 'report' feature?" She

looked through the site's FAQs and terms and conditions, and the only option they gave was to report to the police any illegal activity. "A great lot of help you are."

She decided the best thing she could do was deactivate her account and delete the app. She had no use in her life for a program that cared so little about whether or not they hosted *liars* on their site. But even when the little icon disappeared from her home screen, she wasn't satisfied. Bryce was out there, ready to try to hoodwink the next single woman. It wasn't fair. They deserved to know exactly who he was.

"Hmmm. Maybe this stupid dating site won't do anything to warn other women away from his scam, but I sure can!" Sara said out loud, her magic swirling just under her skin, begging to be used.

Normally, she wouldn't even bother with such a thing, seeking petty revenge on a person whom she had caught in a multitude of lies, but there was something about Bryce that seemed dangerous to the women he sought to be around.

And she couldn't do anything about Rhett's actions, so she might as well do what she could.

Sara printed off Bryce's picture from the dating

site and gathered her supplies, candles, salt, and a few herbs. She went to her spell room and quickly poured the salt into a small circle on her worktable. She placed Bryce's picture in the middle of the circle and tossed a few herbs on top of his image.

Sara thought long and hard about what she wanted to do to teach Bryce a lesson. She didn't want to harm him physically or anything like that. She wasn't that kind of witch. No, what she wanted to do was something harmless enough, but that would make him think twice before he lied again.

The spell had to be something simple. Something easy yet effective. A lightbulb clicked on above Sara's head, and she giggled when the perfect punishment popped into her head.

"Ha! That should teach him a lesson," she laughed, and got to work, chanting:

When he lies with his fingers, let them burn from the effort.

When he lies with his tongue, let his throat bubble and burp.

Sara felt her magic rush through her veins as she poured her energy into the spell. She couldn't help the smile that spread across her face as his picture ignited in the circle of salt. She knew without a doubt it would work, and any time Bryce tried to tell an untruth, he'd be delivered a reminder that would make him think twice.

With the spell completed, Sara felt the usual exhaustion that hit her after a long-distance one such as this spell.

She wanted to clean up after herself, but the salt and candles could wait because a wave of dizziness hit her so hard she needed to sit.

There was no chance for that, though, because Sara heard a noise coming from her backyard. It was a loud thump, followed by a large bang. Like something had crashed into her yard. She ran to the back door and pulled open the slider. Stepping out onto the patio, she couldn't see a thing. She nearly jumped out of her skin when she heard a loud hissing sound right next to her.

It was a large cat, like a Lynx, and it was about to attack her!

The earth seemed to tilt on its axis. Everything around Sara spun with abandon. She felt like she was going to throw up as a sick feeling started to climb up her throat. A sharp pain shot through her body, knocking her to her knees. She cried out for help, but no one answered. Just as she thought she would pass out from the pain, it suddenly stopped as quickly as it had begun.

Am I being attacked? Perhaps the lynx knocked her down, and she hit her head.

But as she looked up, she realized the lynx was nowhere to be seen.

She sat up and caught sight of movement on the lawn. It was the lynx, sprinting away toward the road. Then, it shifted into a man's form before hopping in a nearby car and speeding away.

What the hell? She thought.

She tried to stand and found herself wobbling from side to side. When she looked down at her feet to make sure everything was okay, she nearly passed out when she saw two gray paws where her feet should have been.

"What the actual fuck?" Sara shouted … or at least she tried to, but nothing came out.

Well, that wasn't exactly true. She should have heard her own words. Instead, she heard an animal yipping. It was then that she caught her reflection in the sliding glass door on her back patio. Sara gasped, but again, nothing came out that sounded even remotely human.

Shock tore through her entire body, threatening to consume her mind, body, and soul. Staring back at her was a beautiful grey wolf with white patches and streaks running through her thick fur. But what caught her attention the most was her own eyes staring back at her from the face of a wolf.

"Do you hear something?" Barbara asked Tristan, who was sitting next to her on the couch.

"Yeah, what the hell is that?" he replied, cocking his head to the side, trying to determine what the noise they were hearing was and where it was coming from.

"I have no idea," Barbara said, also cocking her head as Tristan had done. "It almost sounds like someone scratching at the door." Barbara rose from her seat with Tristan following close on her heels in search of an answer.

"It's definitely coming from outside," Tristan said, taking the lead in front of his wife.

"I think you're right," Barbara said just as a whining sound started.

Slowly, Tristan pulled open the front door to see what was making all the noise. They gasped in surprise when they saw a beautiful gray wolf with emerald green eyes staring up at them.

"Well, who do we have here?" Barbara asked. They could tell the difference between a regular wolf and a shifter, and this one was clearly a shifter.

"I have no idea," Tristan replied. "Definitely not someone from our pack."

Even so, Barbara heard him using the pack link to attempt to communicate with the wolf. Sometimes alphas could get through to strange wolves just because of the magnitude of power they held.

No luck. The wolf whined at them and slinked right past them into their home, clearly showing she was in distress.

"Sure! Come right in and make yourself at home," Tristan said, his voice confused but kind.

The wolf did just as Tristan had instructed and

jumped up on the couch. She walked right over to the end, where the table butted it up against it, and proceeded to lap up the water in the glass that had been sitting on the table.

"I guess she was thirsty," Barbara mused. "She must have run a long way."

"This is like the fucking twilight zone. What the hell is going on? You'd think as the alpha, I'd know. But I really don't have a damn clue about anything right now. Do you?" Tristan asked, turning to face his wife.

"Nope. Go fish! You really don't have any idea who this is? Are we being punked by one of our kids or someone else in the pack who thought it would be funny the mess with the alpha?" Barbara shrugged. She acted calm and cool because she had no idea what they were supposed to do with the newcomer.

"If someone put her up to it, I'll bet they are having a good laugh at our expense, but I doubt it. She looks too wild and panicked to be pranking us."

"I think you're right," Barbara said softly, sitting down on the couch next to the strange wolf. "Okay, ma'am, how about you shift back into your human form and talk to us?"

The wolf whined and hopped down from the couch, looking back and forth between Tristan and Barbara in dismay.

"Is it just me, or does she look embarrassed?" Barbara asked.

"Well, I guess there's only one way to figure this out," Tristan said before shifting to his wolf form so he might have a better chance at wolf-wolf communication rather than the strange human-to-wolf non-pack link.

Barbara watched as her husband effortlessly shifted from human to wolf. She loved watching his transformation. He was simply stunning as a wolf. He was much larger than the small gray female who had invaded their home. She had to believe the female had come in peace and meant no harm. It was easy to tell from her demeanor.

He circled the female twice before shifting back to his human form.

"You're not gonna believe this." Tristan ran his fingers through his hair. The look of disbelief was plastered to his hands and face.

"What?" Barbara asked.

"It's Sara!"

"I'm sorry. It sounded like you said that's *Sara*?"

Barbara swore that her eyes bugged out of her damn head. "Like, new witch in town, Sara?"

"Yep! That's exactly what I said," Tristan replied.

"That's impossible. She's not a shifter."

Tristan shrugged, pulling on his clothes. "Well, it's her, alright."

Barbara's head snapped to the small gray wolf. "Sara? Is that really you? How is this possible?"

The wolf trotted over to her and whined again.

"No way! You need to shift back to your human form, and we clearly need to have a chat!" Barbara couldn't believe her eyes. She wouldn't believe it until she saw Sara shift from wolf to human.

The Sara wolf let out a single, sad howl before training her eyes on the ground in front of her.

"Why won't she shift back to her human form?" Barbara asked, turning to Tristan.

Tristan cocked his head and stared at Sara. "I don't think she knows how."

Barbara turned back to Sara to see her nodding her head up and down. "Huh. Good guess, honey. This is way too weird."

Barbara crouched down to be at eye level with Sara. "Listen up, sweetie. All you have to do to shift is to imagine yourself as a human. It's going to feel strange, but you have to allow that magic to overcome you. To swallow you whole. You understand that about magic, right?"

The wolf nodded in agreement.

"Good. Now, don't fight it because if you do, it's going to hurt like hell. Now, take a deep breath and picture yourself in human form. And just remember to follow through with the magic behind it. Don't be scared. Don't panic. You'll be just fine."

The atmosphere in the living room changed. Barbara could feel the shifter magic all around her. She saw Sara's body begin to vibrate. "Just like that. You've got this. Don't fight the magic," she encouraged her friend through the transition.

"Did I do it?" Sara asked before collapsing to the ground.

"Oh my, Tristan! Is she okay?" Barbara cried out as Sara fainted.

"What the hell just happened?" Tristan shouted, lunging for Sara.

"Get her up on the couch," Barbara said before dashing to the bathroom to grab a wet washcloth.

Quickly grabbing the needed supplies, Barbara rushed back to the living room to help her friend.

"Is she okay?" Barbara asked her husband, who stood sentry over Sara.

"She seems to be," he said, backing away as Barbara sat on the couch beside Sara and placed the cold washcloth on her forehead. "Her heartbeat is steady, as is her breathing. I think this whole ordeal was just too much,"

"Sara," she called out, hoping her friend would quickly regain consciousness. She looked back at Tristan. "Can you grab an ice pack?"

"Yeah, I'll get it."

"What happened to you?" Barbara murmured, looking back at Sara. "How did you shift into a wolf?"

Her questions went unanswered. Tristan returned with the ice pack, and she gratefully took it from him. "Would you mind going back to our room and finding a nightgown of mine or a big shirt for her to wear? She won't like waking up naked in a strange place."

He nodded, left, and returned quickly with a big oversized shirt that also happened to be a nightgown. He helped prop Sara up while Barbara managed to get her dressed, and then they settled her back down.

Finally, Sara's eyes fluttered open. She looked

startled as if she were ready to bolt at a moment's notice.

"It's okay, honey. You're safe," Barbara said, running a comforting hand over Sara's arm.

"What? What happened? I had the strangest dream. How did I get here?" Sara asked.

"Here, let me get out of the way so you can sit up. Do you need a drink?" Barbara asked.

"Yeah. Actually, I do. I feel very weak right now," Sara shook as she sat up.

"I'll get you a soda. Something sugary to pep you up," Tristan offered

"Thanks, babe." Barbara sat next to Sara, waiting for an explanation as to the night's events and what led up to Sara showing up at Barbara's house in wolf form.

"Here you go." Tristian returned quickly and handed Sara a can of soda and a glass filled with ice.

"Thanks." Sara set the cup on the table beside her and cracked the can of soda. She skipped the ice and poured half the can down her throat. "Sorry. I don't know what is wrong with me. I've never felt like this before."

"What was your dream about?" Barbara asked

as Sara finished off her soda and opened the second one that Tristan handed her.

"I dreamed that I turned into a wolf. Which is completely crazy, right?"

"Ha! You'd think so," Tristan said, taking a seat in the chair across from the couch.

"Honey," Barbara said before pausing. "It wasn't a dream. You were a wolf."

CHAPTER TWELVE

"Please tell me that you're joking!" Sara squealed. It wasn't some weird dream. She had actually turned into a real live wolf. What was she even supposed to do with that?

"It's okay. It's okay," Barbara tried to soothe her.

It wasn't going to work. Not at all. Not even a tiny bit. Sara's anxiety continued to climb through the roof.

"That's easy for you to say," Sara gasped. "There's nothing okay about any of this! I can't turn into a wolf. I'm a witch! This can't be right!"

Sara rambled on, feeling like she was going to freaking hyperventilate. "How could this happen? Is it because Rhett bit me?"

"Rhett bit you?" Tristan asked, looking to his wife to see if she was just as surprised.

She wasn't since Sara had already revealed this to her. Barbara answered for Sara. "Yes, Rhett claimed her at the scenting ceremony."

"So is that it, then?" Sara asked. "He turned me into a wolf?"

"No, that's not it," Barbara said quickly, turning back to face Sara. "That's not how this works. Mating bites don't turn people … or witches … into shifters. You must have already had it in you."

"What happened?" Tristan asked. "Right before you changed?"

"I heard something outside, so I went to find out what it was," Sara answered. "There was a lynx, I think it was going to attack me, but then I guess I fell. I mean, I was dizzy and weak from casting a spell already, and anyway, the next thing I knew, I fell, and the lynx was running away and turning into a human before they got in their car and left."

"Would you have sensed it if this lynx had hexed you? Cast some spell to turn you into a wolf?"

"Oh yes," Sara nodded her head quickly. "I can sense any magic being used around me, and especially on me. There's no way it had anything to do with the lynx. I think it was just coincidental timing."

"That doesn't sound coincidental at all," Tristan said, pacing the room. "It sounds to me like your wolf came out to protect you when you needed it."

"And you said you were dizzy and weak from casting a spell?" Barbara asked. "So you really were in a state where a latent shifter side might feel compelled forward. Especially …"

"Especially what?" Sara asked.

"Well, especially since you'd just received a mating bite and then denied your mate. The bite probably spoke to your shifter side, and then you turning from Rhett would have vexed your wolf."

"My wolf?" Sara blinked in shock, still trying to absorb everything that was happening.

"I'm calling Rhett," Tristan suddenly announced.

"No!" Sara shouted. "Don't call him. I do not want to see him. Not right now. Maybe not ever."

"You're his mate. He deserves to know what's happening to you," Barbara said gently. "I know you don't want to see him, but our shifter way means we respect mates. It means we *have* to tell him what's happening."

Sara was on the verge of tears. "Please. I don't

know what's going on with me, and I just want to go home and think about this. If you have to tell him, could you at least wait until tomorrow?"

Barbara and Tristan exchanged a look, and finally, Tristan nodded. "I'll wait until tomorrow."

She finally breathed a sigh of relief. "Thank you."

"That's what we're here for," Barbara said, giving her a hug. "We take care of our own, and you're one of us now."

"Do you think my wolf knew that?" Sara asked. "Because I don't remember running away from my house, but somehow I ended up here."

"I think that's a good assumption," Tristan said, finally sitting down on the arm of the couch and looking carefully at Sara. "Now, about the lynx shifter on your property. You felt like he was there to attack you, and it makes sense that your wolf would want to defend you."

"Right," Sara agreed. "But maybe I'm wrong…"

"We're going to assume you're right because we want to be better safe than sorry," Tristan said. "I'm going to call up my tech guy right now and get him out there to install some motion detector cameras and security alarms. I'm also going to go out there with him to see if I can pick up the lynx's scent, see if I can identify them."

Tristan pulled his phone from his pocket and fired off a couple of quick text messages.

"Great. I'll go with you," Sara stood, standing up. It was at that moment she realized she was in a nightgown that wasn't hers. "Oh no, I showed up naked?"

"Well, you showed up in fur," Barbara laughed. "You shifted into a naked human, but don't be embarrassed. Shifters see enough nudity that it doesn't bother us."

"I think you should stay here with Barbara …" Tristan interjected.

"I'm going too!" Barbara stood next to Sara, crossing her arms over her chest.

"I can't talk the two of you into staying here? All things considered?" Tristian asked.

"Nope," they answered in unison.

"Look, I have no idea what we are going to find when we get there. I'd really rather you girls …"

"Don't you dare start with that caveman shit with me," Barbara growled! "You know damn well that we can take care of ourselves. Besides, you'll be there. We'll be perfectly fine."

Sara nodded. "She's a wolf, and I'm a … well, I

don't know what the hell I am right now, but I'm not without my own magic." When this whole damn thing was over, she really was going to have to get to the bottom of things.

"Fine," Tristan said.

"Fine," Barbara agreed.

"Fine," Sara said.

"It's all clear. There's no one here," Tristan said, pulling the sliding glass door closed behind him.

"Any idea who it was?" Barbara asked.

"Definitely a feline shifter," Tristan pulled out one of the dining room chairs and joined the women. "But no one I know of specifically."

"This night keeps getting weirder and weirder," Sara sighed, taking a large gulp of the coffee that was keeping her awake.

"It really does," Barbara agreed. "Are you sure you don't want to spend the night at our house? We have plenty of room for you."

"No, but thank you. This is my home. No one is going to scare me away from it. I'll do a few spells to add some layers of protection on top of the cameras and alarms your guy set up. I'll be fine."

There was no way she was about to be chased out of her home by God only knew what. It wasn't that she didn't trust Barbara and Tristan. She did. Very much so. But she loved her freedom and independence, and she refused to be scared into anything. Right now, more than anything, she needed some time alone to wrap her head around everything.

"Okay, but please, call us if you need anything." Barbara stood and hugged her.

"I will. I promise." She quickly returned the hug and walked them to the front door.

"Lock up as soon as we leave. And don't open your door unless you know who's standing on the other side," Tristan said.

"I won't. I'll be fine."

"You better be," Barbara warned.

"You two should get out of here. I'm sorry I turned your night upside down." She honestly felt bad about dragging them into her mess.

"Hush. I won't hear any kind of talk like that. That's what we're here for. We'd expect you to come to us when you need help," Barbara said, giving her one last hug. "Try to get some rest."

"I will." Sara closed and locked the door the second they stepped over the threshold and headed to their SUV.

Her mind was a total disaster with everything that had taken place, from the hot sex with Rhett to the mating bite, and then the date with Bryce, to the whole shifting into a wolf thing. It was all too damn much. She felt like her head was about to explode.

She padded into the kitchen and grabbed the tea kettle. Filling it halfway, she turned the burner on and grabbed a pack of chamomile tea and her favorite mug, hoping it would help her relax enough to get a few hours of sleep.

Sara nearly jumped out of her skin when the whistle on the tea kettle sounded. Her anxiety really was getting the best of her. That was the last thing she needed, the long spiral into oblivion.

She'd seen it happen to one too many a witch when they lost their way, and she refused to become one of them, no matter how insane every-thing seemed at the moment.

She dipped her tea bag in and out of the steaming water several times before taking a few slow sips of the tea.

"Mmmm. Much better," she said about a

quarter of the way through her cup. She could already feel herself relaxing.

Setting the cup on the counter and flicking the lights off, she headed back to her bedroom to see if she could find the blackness she desperately needed.

SLOWLY OPENING HER EYES, Sara yawned and stretched her arms above her head. She'd been exhausted the night before, and she didn't even remember falling asleep. The second her head hit the pillows, she was out cold without a care in the world … despite how awful the night had ended.

She rolled over and checked her clock.

"Oh no!" Her stress quickly returned when she realized that Vera would be arriving soon for their daily lesson.

She quickly texted the apprentice to let her know that there were new security features around the house, but her key should still work to let her in. Then, Sara jumped out of bed and ran to the bathroom. She flew through her morning shower rituals, realizing that her body was a bit sore.

She thought it must be from the shifting, still partly unable to believe that it had been true and not a crazy dream.

Once done, she threw on the first outfit that she laid her hands on. She slapped on a bit of makeup … she didn't need to scare her apprentice with her natural face … and tied her hair back in a scarf.

Vera was already waiting in the kitchen for her by the time she made it downstairs. Sara was glad the girl had a key to the place, especially when she saw what Vera had been up to.

"Sweet girl, you made coffee!" Sara cried, rushing to the blessed drink that Vera offered her.

"I figured that you might have had a late night," Vera replied with a shrug. "What happened? Why did you need to add the alarms and stuff?"

Sara nodded and sighed. "It's a long story."

Before Sara could find the right words, there was a knock at her door. She excused herself and went to answer it.

"What are you doing here?" she snapped when she opened the door to find Rhett standing there. She immediately tried to close it.

"We need to talk," he said, sticking his boot in the doorway to stop her from slamming it on him.

"No. We really don't." She considered leaving the door and going back to the kitchen, but she didn't want him to follow her in. "You're not welcome here. You need to go."

"I don't know why I let you drive off the other night," he said, pushing the door wider so she had to look at him. "I should have grabbed you and stopped you."

"Because you want to make a habit of forcing me into things against my will?"

His face fell in shame. "Look, Tristan called me this morning and told me what's going on. I'm here to help. We can forget about the … "

"Sara?" Vera's soft voice chimed up behind her and cut off Rhett's words. "I just got a call that something came up, so I'm going to have to cancel for today."

"It's okay, Vera, you don't have to go." Sara looked back at the girl. Certainly, her apprentice was making this up to get out of the awkward situation. "This man was just about to leave."

"Sara, you have to talk to me," Rhett objected.

"No, really, I have something I have to take care of," Vera said, slipping past both Sara and Rhett. "I'll see you tomorrow."

Sara threw up her hands in defeat, walking

away from the front door when she saw Vera drive away.

She went back to her kitchen, to the blessed coffee that still waited for her.

Rhett followed.

Without looking at him, Sara snapped, "Do you have any idea how I spent my night?"

"Tristan told me a bit, yeah."

"Oh, he did?" She was going to take another sip of coffee and realized her cup was empty. Luckily, Vera left more. She poured herself a second cup while she told Rhett, "So he told you that I heard something outside and went to go check? That I then shifted into a wolf and ran to his house out of some instinct, and then they coached me to shift into human form, and I passed the fuck out?"

"Yeah, that's what he told me."

He helped himself to a cup of coffee, and she nearly slapped his hand for it.

But she held back.

Why?

Because I'm glad he's here. Because his presence soothes me in a way that chamomile tea can't. Because he's my mate, and I need him.

Her own thoughts were echoed by the new voice that lived inside her. One she recognized as her wolf. Someone who had been there her whole life but who had been drowned out by all the magic she'd focused on instead.

She shook her head, stopping herself from thinking too much into anything other than her explanation to Rhett. "Anyway, after that, they took me home and verified that I hadn't hallucinated the lynx shifter, and Tristan had all these cameras and alarms set up."

She was still pretty pissed at him but nowhere near as angry as the night of the scenting ceremony. Something inside of her felt almost giddy that he was standing there in front of her, looking hot as hell, wanting to work things out.

"How the fuck did you shift into a wolf?" he asked.

"I have no idea. Trust me, I was just as surprised as you seem to be by the fact that it did happen."

"What did Tristan and Barbara say about it?" he asked.

"That the wolf had to be inside me my whole life, but I was weakened after doing a spell, and she might have sensed the danger from the lynx and came out to save me."

"That's all?" He asked, looking at her closely.

She bit her lip. "They also said that the mating bite might have awakened her … and that shunning you might have displeased my wolf and caused her to come to the surface."

"Ah. I see."

"Yep, now you see. And, now you can go."

He didn't look happy at that, but he also seemed like he was willing to listen. Perhaps seeing that she was okay was enough to allow him to respect her wishes. "We're going to have to talk at some point. You know that, right?"

"I can't do this with you right now." She threw up her hands in exasperation.

"Can't or won't?" he demanded.

"Both!"

"Why?" he inched closer to her, his heat and scent enveloping her.

She slowly backed away from him. "I'm fucking terrified, Rhett. Of you. Of this relationship! Don't you get it? I fell so damn hard and so fucking fast for you … I just can't," Sara shouted as tears slipped from her eyes.

"Why? What's wrong with falling hard and fast for me? Especially when I feel the same way? I love you, Sara. Is that what you need to hear?"

"No. It's not what I need to hear or what I want to hear. I can't!"

"Why?" he demanded

When she didn't answer, he made an assumption. "So you'd rather walk away because you fear what could be?"

"Stop. Just stop. You need to go."

"Not until we talk about this."

Sara steeled her spine and pulled herself together. She couldn't afford to lose her shit right now. "Go."

"Sara, please."

God, he was so freaking hot she couldn't take it. Even when she had just professed her intent to stay away from him, every part of her wanted to kiss him and take away his pain and sadness.

She watched as his muscles flexed with one simple motion. Sweet goodness, she was a goner. Drool pooled in the corners of her mouth. Heat shot straight to her damn core.

Mmm. He's ours, her wolf's voice inside her head said.

Even so, she pointed Rhett to the door.

CHAPTER FOURTEEN

Rhett paced back and forth in front of Sara's Bed and Breakfast. He wanted to march right back in there and yank her into his arms and never let go, but she had locked him out. If he hadn't checked her scent, he would have never believed the story about her shifting into a wolf. But she had, and he did believe her. She had a whole new scent, and it was driving him wild.

Rhett yanked his cellphone from his pocket and hit the speed dial button for his assistant.

"Hi, Mr. Parker," a cheerful woman answered the phone.

"Hi, Kayleigh. Can you do me a favor and move

my morning meeting to tomorrow. Something urgent came up, and I need to go see Tristan."

"I hope everything is okay. Let me know if you need anything."

"I will. Thank you." He kept the call short and sweet. Glancing back at Sara's home one last time, Rhett had to trust that she would be okay while he took care of business. Though she had done an awfully good job of acting like she was indifferent toward him, he knew better. He sensed her wolf *and* that her wolf had an interest in him, to the degree that it was perfectly clear that Sara's wolf considered Rhett her mate.

No matter how hard Sara tried to fight her feelings for him, he would always have her animal in his corner. She might huff and puff and make a big to-do about it, but when it came down to it, the animal inside of her would want her mate by her side no matter what.

That didn't give him a pass on the fact that he had royally screwed up. Nope. Not at all. He was going to have to work ten times harder to convince Sara to give him a second chance, but she *was* his mate, and he wasn't about to walk away.

Even if he had wanted to, it would be physically impossible. His wolf would always long for her.

Now that the animal knew who his mate was, he would always want her, need her, and love her no matter what.

Rhett hopped in his truck and headed for Tristan's house. He needed answers, and his friend was the kind of alpha who could be counted on for some wisdom in times like these.

"I figured I'd see you at some point today," Tristan said, stepping out onto the front porch when Rhett arrived.

"You figured right. I think we need to talk, and Barbara should probably be here as well if she's around," Rhett said.

"Come on in. She just started a fresh pot of coffee," Tristan said, holding the door open.

Rhett didn't know what it was, but the alpha's house always smelled like *home*.

"Well, well, well. Look who we have here," Barbara said, pouring a cup of coffee and putting it on the table for Rhett.

"Good morning to you too," Rhett said, nodding his head in thanks for the drink.

"Have a seat." Tristan nodded at the dining room table before filling up his coffee mug and taking a seat of his own. "I'm guessing you've seen Sara today?"

Rhett nodded. "Did either of you have any idea that she had a shifter hidden inside her?"

He sipped the warm beverage and waited for the alpha to speak. Tristan and Barbara exchanged glances before Barbara answered. "No, we didn't."

"You mean to tell me you had *no* idea?" Rhett asked, finding it hard to believe that the alpha and his wife didn't know about Sara.

"Neither one of us knew because *she* didn't know," Tristan said. "And before you even ask ... The answer is no. I've never seen anything like this before, ever. Not in all my years as a wolf or being an alpha. I don't know why the wolf gene stayed dormant in her for so long. It doesn't make a lick of sense. So, we can't blame Barbara for her meddling. Not this time, anyway."

Tristan laughed, and his wife joined him, but they quickly turned serious again when Rhett asked, "How is any of this even possible?"

"We don't really know," Tristan admitted before nodding to his wife to explain.

"I've spoken to a few other witches, and the most likely scenario is that her shifter gene may have been latent inside of her, buried underneath the magic she'd been honing since she was a child. Your mating bite probably stirred her sleeping wolf, and the next time she used magic, it was like a dam bursting, allowing her wolf to finally step out into the world the moment she was in danger."

His mind was blown. Not only was Sara a wolf, but she hadn't even known about it until last night.

And he hated that she hadn't gone to him for help.

"What did she tell you when you spoke to her?" Tristan asked.

"Not a whole lot, considering I'm in the dog house," Rhett said. "She told me about shifting, but that was it before she kicked me out."

"Good for her," Barbara chuckled. "Sorry, but you know you deserve that. I can't believe you claimed her during the ceremony without clearing it with her first. You're a grown man, and you really let your senses get away from you like that?"

Before he could answer, Tristan came to his defense. "The mating sense is overwhelming for someone, no matter their age. It's not like Rhett's experienced it before and could have been prepared. They got swept up in the moment."

"I wish that was a good enough excuse." Rhett sighed. "The truth is, I messed up big time, and I need to figure out a way to earn Sara's forgiveness.

So I can be there for her now while she's going through this."

"I know you will," Barbara said, her voice softening a bit.

Tristan cleared his throat. "Now, to the other issue at hand."

"What's that?" A surprise wolf shifter and a disgruntled mate were enough. What else could Tristan be waiting to reveal?

"Sara thinks that someone is after her."

"The lynx, right?" Panic rose in Rhett's chest. "Do you think they're going to try coming back?"

"Maybe, maybe not," Tristan said calmly. "It might be that they saw her shift, and now they will think twice about trying anything. Plus, I've had my tech guy install security cameras and alarms."

"It could have been a wild animal." Rhett could hope.

"No, I was there last night, and I distinctly smelled shifter." Tristan shook his head. "Plus, she watched him run off and shift into his human form before getting into his car."

"Did she get a good look at him?" Rhett asked.

"No, he was too far away, and it was too dark."

"Damn." Rhett shook his head and wracked his brain for ideas on who this might be. "Are there some people upset about the new witch in the area? Competing witches or someone loyal to her predecessor?"

Barbara answered. "Not that we know of, and I've been asking around in the witch community."

"Did she come here with any enemies?" Rhett asked. "Students who didn't like their grades or something? I know it's unlikely that she pissed anybody off in the short time she's been here ..."

"Oh, no!" Barbara groaned and cut him off.

"What is it?" Tristan asked.

Rhett's glance flew to Barbara. What was it that she didn't want to say?

She went to the coffee maker, bringing over the carafe and refilling each of their cups before she sat down and took a deep breath.

"I hadn't even considered it because why would he have followed her?" she wondered aloud.

At the word *he*, Rhett bristled. "Who?"

Barbara looked guilty, but she continued. "Sara had been signed up on a dating site before she met you. Well, after what happened between you two, I guess she wanted to try to get over you by going out with someone else."

"What?" Rhett's rage boiled. Not at Barbara or

Sara, but at the idea that someone had dated *his mate* and then followed her back to her home.

Barbara went on, ignoring Rhett's anger. "She met him for dinner, only to find out that he was nothing but a liar, and she called him out on it. You don't think that he would have been so mad at the rejection that he followed her home, do you?"

Neither Rhett nor Tristan answered. They both knew what kind of depraved people lived in this world.

Finally, Rhett asked, "what did the man lie about?"

"Pretty much everything, starting with his age. He spewed some lines about it, like commanding respect from his peers and women if he somehow appeared to be older. She found it really creepy and basically told him to fuck off."

"And the little shit didn't take it well," Tristan assessed.

"I honestly don't know, but I do know one thing, "Barbara said.

"What's that? "Rhett asked.

"In that, Sara isn't the type to mince words," Barbara answered. "My guess is that she probably let him have it, and he likely isn't the type to handle that well. But we must remember that it may not even be him for all we know. I'm just coming up with theories here."

"It's a good theory," Tristan assured her.

"Especially since we don't have anything else to go on." Rhett agreed with Tristan.

He really did need to find a way to get Sara to move past being mad at him so they could figure out what was going on and who this mysterious stalker of hers was. He didn't like the idea of his mate being in danger. It made his wolf antsy, ready to strike out to protect what was theirs.

And it would be much easier to do that if he was welcome on her property.

"I think I'm gonna take a ride over there to see if I can pick up on the scent," Rhett said.

"I'll go with you. It was dark last night, and I'd like to get a better look around in the daylight. Besides, Sara might not kick you out if I'm with you. At least this way, I can explain to her what we are doing and why we are both there." Tristan turned and looked at his wife. "Do you want to go too, or are you good staying here?"

"I'll go too. I think I'd like to sit with Sara for a bit, just to give her someone to talk to."

CHAPTER FIFTEEN

"Hey, Sara. What do you think of this spell?" Vera asked, pointing to a page in the old grimoire that she had been searching through.

"Hmmm." Sara plucked her bejeweled pink eyeglasses that were perched on top of her head and slid them over her eyes, hoping she would finally be able to decipher the tiny fuzzy letters on the yellowed page.

"Yeah. That sure looks like the spell I was talking about. That should do it," Sara said, glad she could help Vera find the right spell, and she was also glad that Vera had returned shortly after she'd left. Turns out, she wanted to give Rhett and Sara time to talk and had decided picking up some breakfast would be a good way to waste a little time.

"Yay! I'm so excited to try this. Thank you." Vera beamed up at her.

"You are very welcome. So, now you're off for the rest of the day?" Sara asked.

"Yes, my boyfriend and I are going out of town. We've been looking forward to it for a while now." Vera beamed, and Sara couldn't help but wish she had that same kind of peace and love in her relationship with Rhett.

"Have fun. I'll see you next week."

She escorted Vera to the front door and then carefully locked it behind her. Having the apprentice with her that morning had soothed her nerves, and she wasn't looking forward to being alone again, despite what she'd told Rhett, and regardless of how many security cameras were now around her house, that she could look at on her phone app.

She'd barely made it back to the couch when her phone chimed with an alert from the motion detector, and then her doorbell rang. She pulled up the live video feed and saw Barbara was at her doorstep.

"Hey! What are you doing here?" Sara asked when she opened the door.

Barbara held up two takeout bags. "I thought I'd bring you some lunch and keep you company."

Sara heard the unstated *and check up on you,* but she appreciated it all the same.

"Come on in."

"You might want to turn your phone on silent," Barbara said as she walked over to set the bags down on the dining room table.

"Why?"

"Tristan wants to go over the property again, see if he can pick up anything in the daytime that he might have missed at night."

"Okay." Sara nodded, pulling out her phone and switching it to silent.

"And Rhett is with him."

Sara's eyes flicked to the back window, and she caught sight of the two men walking around back there.

"I hope this is okay with you," Barbara said, pulling the food out of the bags.

"It's perfectly fine," Sara assured her.

Once they were seated and had taken their first bites, Barbara asked the question, "So, how are you today?"

Sara shrugged. "I've been thinking a lot about who I am. Things like, I always thought I loved the woods and outdoors because my witch nature drank it in, but really, there was a wolf inside who craved it."

"At least they were compatible with that," Barbara reasoned.

"Yeah, but maybe if my sleeping wolf had been a little *less comfortable,* it would have come out sooner and demanded attention."

"Maybe." Barbara chewed another bite of the burger before adding, "But I really wouldn't suggest dwelling on stuff like that. Dealing with the *now* is going to be a lot more productive and healthier for you."

"Yeah, you're right." Sara sighed. "It's not like I can find any answers from my parents. My mother passed on long ago, so it's not like I could call her and ask her about why I suddenly shifted into a freaking wolf. And I never knew my dad, so maybe that's where the gene came from."

"Could be," Barbara agreed.

"Either way, I have a lot of catching up to do when it comes to being up to speed on the knowl-edge of being a shifter. I am like a middle-aged toddler when it comes to my wolf. It feels like the most ridiculous thing ever when you consider my witch expertise and the fact that I'm a mentor."

Barbara took her hand. "You're older and wiser, which means you'll catch on quickly. And you have Tristan, me, and the whole pack here to help you."

A thud outside had Sara spinning to look. The guys were doing something on the porch. "He came to see me this morning, and I kicked him out."

"I know," Barbara said. "He came to our place after and told us."

"I'm still really pissed at him, yet, there's this part of me that wants to get over it and forgive him."

"Of course, you feel that way. He's your mate."

Sara frowned, considering the words. "I don't really know a lot about my wolf, I feel like she's a stranger to me, but I *can* feel her certainty that Rhett *is* our mate."

"Are you okay?" Barbara asked.

"I don't know. So much has gone on in such a short amount of time. Moving here, meeting Rhett, having him give me a mating bite ..."

"The intruder, the shift, the run to my house, the passing out ..." Barbara finished her sentence for her.

Sara watched the men leave the porch. Then, they shifted into their wolf forms and took off toward the woods. "I guess they're looking for more clues out there."

It wasn't a minute later when her door was busted down, and an angry man charged in. Both women stood in alarm while the wild man shouted, "What did you do to me?"

"Bryce! What are you doing here? What do you mean?" Sara asked.

Bryce looked as if he had seen better days. He had a black eye and a busted lip, and his clothes looked like they hadn't been washed in weeks. He also looked like *he* hadn't been washed in weeks, though she'd just been on her date with him the night before.

"What did you do to me? I went home last night, and all these weird things started happening to me, and when I told my friend about it, they informed me that you were a witch, and you hexed me."

"When you went home last night? Was that before or after you came around here trying to break in and attack her?" Barbara instantly came to Sara's defense.

Bryce looked absolutely crazed like he was off his rocker. That was when Sara noticed a large blade in his hand. She didn't know what he planned on doing with that weapon, and she sure didn't want to find out.

"Bryce, I can explain. Just calm down. Put the knife down," Sara said, quickly glancing at Barbara, who was staring out the window toward the woods and where their men had disappeared into it.

"Whatever you did, you need to undo it," he demanded, inching closer to where she stood.

"Hold on a minute!" Barbara finally looked away from the window and faced Bryce. "You smell like a shifter. Lynx, to be exact, am I correct?"

"Yeah, why?"

"Because that means you should be able to smell on both of us that we're wolves."

"She's not a wolf," he said, pointing to Sara. Then, he took a moment, considering her scent, before adding, "Well, she sure wasn't when we went on our date, so you must be doing something to make it seem like she's a wolf now."

"Were you not here yesterday and saw a wolf?" Barbara asked, to Sara's surprise.

"That must have been *you*," Bryce accused.

"I promise you, it was not," Barbara stated in

such a cool tone that it brought goosebumps to Sara's arms.

The woman held such a reserved, awe-inspiring power without raising her voice at all.

"She smells like a wolf now," Barbara continued. "And it's not a trick. She *is* a wolf, and she didn't hex you."

"I don't know how she did it, damn it! But she had to have because everything went to hell after meeting her. I know it was her! It has to be."

"I'm a wolf! Not a witch, you moron!" Sara lied, hoping to keep him tied up in the debate long enough that she could come up with a plan. Bryce was growing angrier by the second, and she had to do something before someone got hurt.

"Seriously, have you ever seen someone who is both wolf and witch?" Barbara continued the lie.

"I should have known your pack had something to do with this! Don't think I know about the shit that goes on here. I may not live here, but everyone whispers about those freaks in Blue Creek," Bryce shouted.

"Please, what do you know about us? That we are loyal to each other? That we protect our own?" Barbara rolled her eyes.

"Enough! You'll be the first one to die, and I'll

make her watch!" Bryce shouted as he began a full-on charge toward Barbara.

"No!" Sara shouted before whispering a quick chant. She flung her arms toward Bryce, sending all of the magic she could muster into a blue fireball that landed squarely on his chest. He bounced off the dining room wall and landed on the floor with a sickening thump.

"Wow!" Barbara cheered, turning toward Sara. "That was some quick thinking! And impressive!"

Just then, her back door was busted down, and Tristan and Rhett tumbled in.

They assessed the situation and then looked at Barbara and Sara. "I see we're too late."

Every muscle in Sara's body itched to run into Rhett's arms. Her instinct, or her wolf, egged her on, and she pleaded with Sara to go to their mate. He looked so damn worried. She fought tooth and nail, willing herself against it.

"And I now need to replace *two* doors," Sara mumbled, leaving the dining room for the safety of the kitchen, allowing the men to deal with Bryce's limp form.

Barbara followed her. "I let Tristan know what was happening through the pack link."

"We ran back here as fast as we could," Tristan added.

"I guess we could have taken our time," Rhett said, crouching down to take Bryce's pulse.

"I take it that this is Bryce?" Tristan asked.

"It is," Barbara answered before turning to Sara. "What in the world did your hex do to make him come undone like this?"

Sara smiled, despite the situation. "His fingers would tingle and burn every time he tried to type a lie, and his throat would fill with bubbles and burps when he tried to speak one."

"Damn." Tristan's word spoke for everyone as he leaned in close to examine Bryce.

"But honestly, I don't regret it. He deserved it," Sara crossed her arms over her chest.

"Oh, I'm not saying that he didn't deserve it." Tristan stood, shaking his head. "He did. I've kicked this man and his roaming clowder out of our territory more times than I care to admit."

"Wait! You know him?" Barbara turned to face her husband.

"Not him in particular. Otherwise, I would have recognized his scent last night, but he looks similar enough to be at least cousins to that cougar shifter who was giving some of the girls a hard time a few years ago."

"You mean the cougar who beat the hell out of Andrea during some sick sex game of his?" Barbara asked.

"That's the one," Tristan said before stepping to the door, where a team of his enforcers had shown up. "Take him away. I'll deal with him later."

CHAPTER SIXTEEN

Barbara and Tristan left, and Sara couldn't stop looking at Rhett.

"If I'd only not freaked out about the mating bite, none of this would have happened," she admitted, feeling like a fool.

"If I'd only have controlled myself and not given you that bite, none of this would have happened."

"I guess we both did something stupid," she said.

"No!" He rushed over to her, pulling her into his arms, and she let him.

It felt so good to rest her head against his chest that it was a real effort to remember why she'd been upset with him in the first place.

"Sara, I'm sorry I did something that upset you, but I can't say I'm sorry that I claimed you. Especially if it in any way helped to wake your wolf."

"Because you prefer me as a shifter?" she asked, pulling back to look at his face.

"No! Because you were going to be attacked by Bryce's lynx while you were weak from casting your spell. He could have really hurt you, but your wolf came out to protect you. *That* is what I'm most thankful for."

"I suppose that is something," she mused. Looking at her handsome mate, she could hardly remember the anger she'd felt just a day ago. That human part of her that was offended is gone, and now her wolf just told her, *of course, he should have claimed me.*

Even this morning, when she'd kicked him out, her wolf had protested. She had been completely against it.

And now her wolf was done being pushed to the back, done allowing the witch and the human to have center stage. Now, her wolf was going to claim what was hers.

"What is it?" Rhett asked, looking at her closely. "Is something wrong?"

She shook her head. "Come with me."

She walked him to her bedroom, pulling off her clothes as she did. He undressed too and kissed a path down the valley of her breasts to her stomach. His tongue dipped into her belly button before continuing further south to the juncture between her thighs.

"Oh!" she moaned, her legs falling open. "I can't think of a better way to celebrate our reunion," she said as his tongue landed on her clit. She fell back on the bed, and her fingers tunneled through his hair, her hips rocking up to meet each swipe of his tongue.

He licked and kissed and sucked her clit into his mouth, driving her toward her climax. The second he slid two fingers deep inside of her and began moving them in and out of her, her orgasm crashed over her and sent her zooming off to the stars.

Just as her body was coming down from its high, Rhett positioned himself between her legs and palmed his cock.

"I want you, Sara," he said, pressing his cock against her entrance.

"Take me. I'm yours," she said.

He drove deep inside of her with one quick flick of his hips. Once he was fully seated, balls deep, he stretched her arms above her head and began slowly pumping in and out of her.

"I want you forever. I want you to be my mate by choice, not by force." His voice was thick and heavy.

Her wolf shouted inside her head, demanding that she make her claim on this man.

"Yes!" she cried out, using her newfound shifter strength to flip him over. She settled on top of him, riding him as she bent over to touch her teeth to his collarbone.

Do it! Now, her wolf shouted in her head.

She didn't resist. She wrapped her arms around his neck and struck as fast and as hard as he had. As she did it, she reached the most intense climax she had ever felt.

Her entire body shook, and her limbs trembled. More pleasure than she had ever thought possible crashed over her. But it was more than just the pleasure. Something inside of her clicked, opening a whole new world. She saw her future with Rhett flash before her eyes. Everything that she had ever wanted out of her life now appeared in her mind, shocking her to her very core.

It's the mating connection, her wolf said. *He is ours, and we are his. Forever!*

Sara's heart filled with that knowledge as she leaned over to kiss him, and he returned it.

"I love you, Sara. I don't know what I'd ever do without you."

"I love you too. So damn much," she said in between kisses.

Her heart was filled with love and excitement for their future together. She had never known what true happiness was until she met Rhett.

While most women wished more than anything to turn back the clock and reverse the years, Sara was the exact opposite. She was loving her magical mid-life, where everything just seemed to get better.

She had found her mate, discovered her wolf, and she was beyond happy with her new position as witch mentor.

Yeah, you couldn't pay her to go back to her youth.

The End.

ABOUT THE AUTHOR

New York Times and USA Today Bestselling Author

Hi! I'm Milly Taiden. I love to write sexy stories featuring fun, sassy heroines with curves and growly alpha males with fur. My books are a great way to satisfy your craving for paranormal romance with action, humor, suspense and happily ever afters.

I live in Florida with my hubby, our son, and our fur babies: Speedy, Stormy and Teddy. I have a serious addiction to chocolate and cake.

I love to meet new readers, so come sign up for my newsletter and check out my Facebook page. We always have lots of fun stuff going on there.

SIGN UP FOR MILLY'S NEWSLETTER FOR LATEST NEWS!

http://eepurl.com/pt9q1